MY PERFECT LIFE

Books by the same author

Confessions of a
Teenage Drama Queen

Tall, Thin, and Blonde

The Boy of My Dreams

MY PERFECT LIFE

DYAN SHELDON

CANDLEWICK PRESS
CAMBRIDGE, MASSACHUSETTS

Copyright © 2002 by Dyan Sheldon

First edition 2002

Library of Congress Cataloging-in-Publication Data

Sheldon, Dyan.
My perfect life / Dyan Sheldon. —1st ed.
p. cm.
Summary: Ella has no interest in running for class president at her suburban
New Jersey high school, but her off-beat friend Lola tricks her into challenging
the rich and overbearing Carla Santini in a less-than-friendly race.
ISBN 0-7636-1839-X
[1. Interpersonal relations—Fiction. 2. High schools—Fiction.
3. Schools—Fiction. 4. Elections—Fiction.] I. Title.
PZ7.S54144 Myp 2002
[Fic]—dc21   2001058118

2 4 6 8 10 9 7 5 3

Printed in the United States of America

This book was typeset in Amasis MT.

Candlewick Press
2067 Massachusetts Avenue
Cambridge, Massachusetts 02140

visit us at www.candlewick.com

I

MY PERFECT LIFE

The first time Lola came to my house, she threw herself on my bed with an unstifled cry. "My God, Ella, is there anything you don't have?" She wasn't just asking a question; she was declaiming.

I said, "Lola?"

She didn't hear me.

Her arms waved and her jewelry rattled. "Your own phone . . . your own television . . . your own video . . . no siblings to gnaw away at your privacy . . ."

"Lola?"

She propped herself on her elbows and gave the radiator a look usually reserved for religious statues. "And temperature control!"

Lola's bedroom was really a sun porch and wasn't equipped with heat.

"Lola?" I said again.

She looked at me, but she still wasn't listening. "You don't know how lucky you are, Ella Gerard. If you changed places with me for just one day—just one day of the slave labor, bourgeois insensitivity, and soul-sucking harassment that is my miserable lot—you'd realize how incredibly lucky you are."

I knew I was lucky—people have been telling me how lucky I am for as long as I can remember—but I didn't really want to hear it again. Not then. I'd heard my mother's car pull into the driveway. Any minute now she might come upstairs to look for me. I figured I could get my mother over the hurdles of Lola's black cape and nose ring, but if she saw what Lola was doing to the bed, she might go into cardiac arrest. Not only was Lola rumpling the covers, but her shoes were actually touching them, too. My mother wasn't that crazy about shoes on the carpet, never mind the bed.

"Lola!" I didn't mean to shout. Shouting could bring my mother running. The only time my parents raised their voices was when there was a lot of other noise or they were far away and they wanted to be heard.

Lola caught her breath. "What?"

"Could you please get off the bed?"

Lola laughed. "What?"

"Could you please get off the bed?" I glanced over my shoulder, half expecting to see my mother in the doorway, smiling with disapproval.

Instead of getting up, Lola leaned back on the pillows. "What for?"

I had to stop myself from going over and yanking her off. "Because my mother doesn't like anyone sitting on the beds." I'd gone from shouting to whispering. Just in case my mother was lurking outside.

Lola, however, doesn't have what you would call an obedient nature. She's not the person rules are made for; she's the person who breaks them. Repeatedly.

"Why not?"

"She just doesn't." Lola was staring at me in a way that made me uncomfortable. "She has a thing about beds."

Now Lola was really curious. "What kind of thing?"

The whole truth was that my mother had a thing about more than beds. If we got into that, we could be at it for hours.

"She's just a very neat and tidy person," I explained. I hoped Lola couldn't tell that my palms were sweating. "She doesn't like the beds messed up."

Lola laughed. "I'm not messing it up. I'm just sitting on it."

"No, you're not. You're messing it up." I wasn't shouting, but I was a little shrill. "*And* your shoes are on the duvet."

One Lola Cep eyebrow rose. Inquisitively. "What is she? Obsessive-compulsive?"

I didn't like the sound of that.

"Of course not. She's just neat and tidy. Now will you please get off?"

"I just don't see what the big deal is," said Lola. She was being deliberately stubborn. I could tell because her voice sounded totally reasonable. "We can straighten it out later. She'll never know."

3

"She will know. My mother has a very special way of making—"

"Your mother makes your bed?" Lola looked as if disbelief might strangle her.

I thought she meant instead of the housekeeper. "Mrs. Wallace can't meet my mother's standards, either. She doesn't make the edges straight enough. My mother likes straight edges."

It was an unnecessary explanation. Lola was still harping on about the fact that I had room service.

"You don't even have to make your own bed?" Lola flopped back against the pillows, her arms stretched toward the ceiling. "O ye gods! Did I get born into the wrong family or what? I don't believe it. You don't even have to make your own bed."

My mother's voice rose up the stairs. "Ella? Is someone with you?"

She meant was Carla Santini with me.

I opened the door and stuck my head into the hall. "Hi, Mom," I called. "I brought Lola home. Remember I told you about Lola? The new girl?"

"Lola?" I'd lived with Marilyn Gerard for fifteen years; I could hear the disappointment in her voice. "Well, come on down and I'll fix you a snack."

Lola sat up. "This is a joke, right? Your mother doesn't really fix your snacks . . ."

I shut the door.

"She doesn't have a job like your mom," I reminded

her. "Taking care of me and my dad and the house is what she does."

Lola rolled her eyes. "Good Lord!" she cried. "Is this Dellwood, New Jersey, or Stepford?"

After that Lola was always asking me questions about my parents—though not nearly as many as they asked about her. *Did they fight? Did they pick on me? Did they nag? Did they . . . Did they . . . Did they . . . ?* They didn't. Everything my parents did was right.

"Your life can't be this perfect," Lola kept saying. "The odds are against it."

No matter what the odds, though, up until I met Lola, I did have a perfect life.

My parents were perfect parents. We lived in Woodford, a perfect and exclusive community, in a perfect town, in a perfect world. I had perfect friends, went to a perfect school, and did perfect things. I was about nine before I realized that not everyone had their own swimming pool and Jacuzzi—it came as quite a shock.

By the time Lola Cep landed at Dellwood High, I was pretty much bored out of my mind. I couldn't see that anything would ever change. I'd finish high school with an excellent academic record, and then I'd go to some perfect college, and then I'd have some perfect career, and eventually I'd marry someone like my father and live in a place just like the one I'd grown up in, and be just like my mother. There were days when it didn't really seem worth the effort to get up in the morning.

But then Lola moved (extremely unwillingly) to Dellwood (the wilderness) from New York City (the very heart and soul of the civilized world), and things started to change. For the first time in my life, I could imagine living another way; being someone else. I didn't know what that other way of living was yet; but at least I knew it existed.

None of us at Dellwood High had ever seen anyone like Lola Cep before. Well, maybe in movies, but not in real life. Lola saw herself as a creative force that would "shine like a lighthouse in the dark and dull suburban night," but that's not how everyone else saw her. Everyone else just saw her as bizarre. Or possibly crazy. She didn't dress like the rest of us, or talk like the rest of us, or act like the rest of us—and her family wasn't like ours, either. Her mother had three children and no husband, which caused quite a few eyebrows to rise. Lola's mother didn't have lunch with the other mothers, or do volunteer work like the other mothers, or play golf like the other mothers, either. Lola's mother was a potter who wore old clothes, drove an old car, and stuck chopsticks in her hair. Lola called her Karen.

At Dellwood High, we were used to kids being bizarre in a quiet, nerdy way, but there was nothing quiet or nerdy about Lola. Lola was bizarre like Salvador Dali was bizarre. You know, outrageous, loud, and larger than everybody else's life. To tell you the truth, I think that everyone except Carla Santini was a little afraid of Lola. Carla just loathed her on sight. I figure it was something genetic.

6

I decided to make friends with Lola for three reasons:

1. Since Carla Santini dumped me when we started high school, I didn't really have any close friends.

2. On her very first day at school, Lola stood up to Carla Santini, which in Dellwood is the equivalent of David knocking out Goliath with a pebble. Carla is beautiful, intelligent, wealthy, and the most popular girl in the school (especially with herself). To balance out these positive qualities, Carla is also domineering, manipulative, calculating, opportunistic, and secure in the knowledge that she was God's special project—and that for her He got an A. In the fifteen years I'd known Carla Santini, no one so much as thought of standing up to her.

3. I felt sorry for Lola. She was like E.T., surrounded by aliens and longing to go home. Only Lola didn't end up in Elliot's back yard; she ended up in Carla Santini's back yard. She might as well have crash-landed in hell.

I don't want you to get the wrong idea . . . I'm not saying that Lola ruined my perfect life; she does have a remarkable amount in common with a nuclear bomb, but she didn't do that. Lola was a catalyst; she caused change.

Change didn't ruin my perfect life, either. It didn't even make it possible for it to be ruined; that was already happening anyway. But change affected the way I reacted when everything started crumbling around me.

And for that I absolutely, definitely, and positively blame Lola Cep.

2

Lola and I Have a Conversation
about the School Elections

Lola and I were in the library that afternoon. We'd found the books we wanted and were waiting for Mrs. Hawley, the librarian, to check them out.

Mrs. Hawley handed me my stack. "I hear your friend Carla Santini's running for president of the student body, Ella. Are you going to be helping her with her campaign?"

It was a long time since Carla Santini and I had been friends, but I couldn't expect Mrs. Hawley to know that. Mrs. Hawley pretty much stayed in the library, safe from the seething social jungle of Dellwood High.

I put my books in my bag. "No. No, I'm not."

Lola didn't say anything. This time. Mrs. Hawley once threw her out for launching into an impassioned rendition of Hamlet's soliloquy in the reading room, so she tended to control herself in the library.

But as soon as we got outside, Lola had plenty to say.

She flung one arm across her forehead. I'm not always sure which actress in which film Lola is modeling herself on, but this time I had a hunch it was Bette Davis. She's a big Bette Davis fan.

"Why didn't you tell me?" wailed Lola. "Why am I always the last to know?"

I was writing down the date my library books were due back in my planner so I wouldn't forget and wasn't totally listening. "Tell you what?"

"The school election, of course. Why didn't you tell me it was imminent? Were you saving it for a surprise?"

I blinked, confused. "I guess I thought you knew."

"You thought I knew?" Lola had replaced the velvet cape she wore in the winter with a turquoise shawl for the spring. It flapped up and down with her arms like wings. "I haven't spent my whole life in Deadwood, like you, Ella. I'm not steeped in every minuscule tradition. How could I possibly know a thing like that?"

"Because it happens at the same time every year." I stuck my planner back in my bag. "And you were here last spring."

She frowned. "It happened last year?"

"That's right. Same time; same place."

"But I'd only just arrived," said Lola. She swung one end of her shawl over her shoulder. "As you well know, at that time I was very deeply traumatized by being dragged out of my spiritual home and into the waste-land of suburbia. You couldn't possibly expect me to remember something as tediously mundane as a student election."

We headed toward the bike rack. There were only two bikes locked to it: Lola's and mine. Everyone else either had a car or a chauffeur.

"If it's so tediously mundane, then why do you care?"

Lola gasped. Presumably in horror. "Why do I *care*? You're asking me why I *care*?"

I stopped walking. Lola often makes me feel as if I've come into the movie after it started.

"I've missed something, haven't I?" I asked.

Most people just sigh—you know, quickly and quietly—but Lola heaves her sighs all over the place like she's Superman and they're boulders. It has something to do with her thespian soul.

"Oh, for God's sake, Ella. I should think that it's obvious—especially to you." And with that, she stalked off, her bangles clattering and her shawl flapping.

And suddenly it was obvious. It was so obvious that I was surprised I hadn't been expecting it. I guess I just assumed that because Lola considered politics beneath the creative soul, it was one theater where she would be willing to let Carla Santini take center stage. How naive can you be?

I practically had to run to catch up with her.

"You can't be serious," I gasped. "You're not actually suggesting that *you're* planning to run against Carla for president, are you?"

Lola was already unlocking her bike. She eyed me over one shoulder, aloof and cool. "And why not?"

There was one really obvious answer to this question: because Carla Santini would decimate her. All Carla had to do was remind everyone that Lola was not only an outsider, but an outsider who was on record as being a major liar as well, and the student body would close ranks. It's something they're good at. Plus, Carla would have the time of her life doing it.

But there was an equally obvious reason why I wasn't going to mention this to Lola just then. I knew Lola well. Telling her that she couldn't run against Carla because Carla would grind her into powder would be like waving a hunk of bloody antelope at a hungry lion; she wouldn't be able to resist.

"Why not?" I pretended to consider this question thoroughly. "Well, let's see . . . For one thing, you're totally uninterested in politics and school government—"

"Not if Carla Santini's planning to run, I'm not," Lola informed me. "That changes things."

"I don't see that it changes anything . . ." I had to be careful what I said. You can't simply tell Lola not to do something, because she'll have done it before you've finished your sentence. You have to let her convince herself. "You're an actor, not a politician. You don't want to waste your talent on something you're not interested in." I gave her a glance. "Something so crass."

Lola stood up. "Well, no, of course, I don't. Acting is my passion and my very life. But the two aren't totally incompatible—"

I cut in before she started listing all the successful actors who had gone on to be successful politicians.

"But it would depress you. I mean, what if you have so much to do as president that you can't even be in the play next year?"

I figured I had her with that one. Lola would rather be imprisoned in Mexico than not be in the school play.

Lola waved this objection away as if it were a gnat. "Oh, that's not a problem. While I'm busy with rehearsals, you can take over my duties."

My jaw dropped. "*Me?* How did I get into this?"

"Well, you'll run as my vice president, of course! And, as vice president, it'll be your job to step in when I'm busy. You know, like when the president of the United States gets impeached or something like that. That's what the vice president's for."

For someone who'd only just learned about the election, she'd certainly thought it all out pretty quickly.

"But, Lola—"

"There are no buts." Lola struck a defiant pose. It was either Joan of Arc or Scarlett O'Hara. "I can't let Carla get the presidency. She'll only use it to extend her tyrannical hold over the minds and hearts and souls of our fellow students. Carla doesn't understand about democracy. The election's just a formality to her. She thinks she should rule by divine right. We owe it to the students of Dellwood High to give them a real government." She threw back her head and raised an arm in the air. The effect was a little less impressive than she intended, since she still had her bike lock in her hand. "One that is based on freedom and creativity, not oppression and conformity."

I backed my bike out of the rack. "I don't think there's

much risk of Carla setting up a dictatorship. The student president's just a figurehead—you know, like the queen of England. She doesn't really do anything, either."

"But she could," argued Lola. "Prince Charles is always getting into trouble for doing stuff. The monarchy, like anything else, is what you make it."

I said, "But—"

Lola rattled her bike lock. "I'm not thinking of myself; I'm thinking of everyone else. The people need me!" cried Lola. "That's all that matters when the last curtain falls."

Personally, I doubted that the people were ready for Lola. At least not the people of Dellwood High.

"You think it might help you play Lear, don't you?" I asked. One of Lola's ten major life ambitions is to play Lear, preferably at the Globe Theatre in London.

"Not just Lear. There's the Richards to think of, too."

I was more concerned with the incredible potential for pain and stress Lola running for student president would mean.

Lola again raised her bike lock toward the sky. "'A horse! A horse! My kingdom for a horse!'" she shouted.

And not just for me. Lola was going to need a lot more than a horse once Carla Santini was through with her.

"'Mine honour is my life; both grow in one; Take honour from me, and my life is done!'"

Exactly, I thought; *that's exactly what Carla will do. And all the king's horses, and all the king's men, would never put Lola back together again.*

It was then that I finally remembered something that was guaranteed to stop all argument about the election once and for all. I almost laughed out loud.

"I just thought of something," I said instead.

Lola asked, "What?"

I even managed not to smile. "You can't run."

Lola laughed. It was a Meryl Streep laugh, throaty and surprised. "Can't win? *I* can't win?"

"I didn't say you can't *win,*" I explained, though that was probably true, too. "I said you can't *run.*"

Lola pointed her bike lock in my direction. "What do you mean I can't run?"

"I mean you can't run. Presidential candidates have to have served at least one term as a homeroom representative. It's a rule."

"Are you sure?"

"Positive. It's in the school constitution."

I figured that was the end of it.

Even Lola couldn't get around that.

14

3

Lola and I Have a Second Conversation about the School Elections

Carla Santini was the first person to declare her nomination for president of the student council. No surprise there.

And probably the only person who was surprised at how quickly Carla handed in her petition of fifty names supporting her candidacy was Dr. Alsop, the principal, who was still in the parking lot when she gave it to him.

By the time the first bell rang, Carla's henchmen already had posters up all over the school. The posters featured a large studio photograph of Carla and the slogan: SANTINI—YOU KNOW SHE'S THE BEST. Although Dr. Alsop applauded Carla's enthusiasm, he made her take them down until the campaign officially began the next Monday.

Lola and I were sitting on the grass in front of the library, determinedly avoiding any talk of the election by discussing *Oedipus Rex* while we ate our lunch. We were doing Greek drama in English. Mrs. Baggoli, our English teacher, says you can't appreciate Western literature without an understanding of Greek drama.

Lola, naturally, loves Greek drama, especially the tragedies, but I was finding the Greeks a little gloomy and depressing.

"How can you say that?" wailed Lola, her voice loud and her gestures large and—because of her bracelets—noisy. She was wearing a lot of scarves that day and about six different dangling earrings, which made her look like some kind of ancient priestess—though not particularly Greek. "Can't you feel their passion? Their thirst for life? Their intimate knowledge of the nature of the universe?"

There were quite a few people nearby, but nobody even glanced over. They were all pretty used to Lola by then.

"I don't see what passion and an intimate knowledge of the universe have to do with it." I unwrapped my dessert, which looked like it might be solid sugar. My mother was doing an advanced course in Asian cooking. "Poor Oedipus. He never had a chance."

"Speaking of losers," said Lola, "there's someone else who doesn't have a chance."

Morty Slinger was loping toward us, his nomination petition in his hand. Morty's glasses are held together with neon-colored tape, and he always wears a suit that doesn't fit (not him, at least), yet he has SAT scores that look like the combined national debts of Nicaragua and Brazil. Morty was the only person either brave or foolish enough to run against Carla Santini. It was enough to break your heart.

Morty loomed over us. It was like being accosted by an accountant. He cleared his throat and shuffled from one foot to the other. "I wondered if you two would sign my nomination petition. I only need forty more names."

"Gee," I said. "Only forty."

"I can't believe you're doing this," said Lola. She gave him a sympathetic smile. "I didn't realize you had a masochistic streak."

"I consider it a defiant gesture." Morty squatted beside her. "You know, like when you went against Carla for the lead in the school play."

"There is a difference, though," said Lola. "Let's not forget that I got the lead. Barring divine intervention, you have less chance of winning against the Santini than of becoming a ballerina."

But Morty isn't just a brilliant mathematician and scientist; there's a touch of the philosopher in him, too.

"I can but try." He sighed. "Somebody has to. If no one else volunteers for this suicide mission, she won't even break a fingernail campaigning. She'll just walk into the presidency the same way she walks into everything else."

Lola took another bite of her apple. "Carla really should be living in South America. She was born to be a military dictator."

"She practically is." Morty shrugged. "I just wish a few people out of our class had ever heard of me. I'm like the invisible valedictorian." He glanced at Lola.

"Now if it were you—everybody knows you. You're famous at Dellwood."

He meant *infamous*.

Lola, however, was already shaking her head. "It can't be me. I know Ronald Reagan was both an actor and a politician, but he wasn't really very good at either. *I,* however, am destined to be a great actress. I can't waste my talent on the crass and tawdry world of politics."

Morty gave her a look. "You mean because of the Sidhartha incident? You figure Carla would use it to turn you into victory confetti?"

Lola laughed. I have to hand it to her: she definitely has promise as a politician as well as an actor.

"Oh, please . . . The Sidhartha incident, as you call it, just happened to be a major personal triumph for me and Ella."

Despite, among other things, being taken into police custody, I thought the Sidhartha incident a major personal triumph, too—in a roundabout kind of way.

"Lying Lola," murmured Morty.

But it did have a dimension of public humiliation.

Lola shook her head and her earrings clattered. "That was nothing but character assassination. It was Carla who was lying, not me. Ella and I went, and saw, and conquered."

Morty, however, isn't at the top of our class for nothing. He tapped his pen against his petition thoughtfully.

"But Carla does have a lot on you, doesn't she? And what she doesn't have she could make up." He smiled warily in Lola's direction. "I mean, there's not much people wouldn't believe about you after that."

I wanted him to shut up. If he didn't stop, he was going to end up goading her into action.

Lola gave him one of her scathing Bette Davis looks. "I'm not afraid of Carla Santini, and everyone knows it." She said it quite loudly. "And besides, that was eons ago."

It was a month or two before.

The Sidhartha incident happened around the time of the school play. Because she was so furious at losing the lead in *Pygmalion* to Lola, Carla made a big deal about being invited to Sidhartha's farewell concert and the party after it. Sidhartha was our favorite band. Not one to ignore an impossible challenge, Lola immediately announced that she and I had been invited, too. Everyone knew Lola was lying. Which was why Carla Santini was able to convince everyone that we hadn't been at the party, when in fact we were. After the police released us.

"So why don't you run, then?" asked Morty. "Forget Reagan. Clint Eastwood never stopped acting even when he was mayor of Carmel. And he directs."

Lola was shaking her head, sadly and with regret. "I can't," she repeated. "I'd be torn in two. A house divided against itself cannot stand."

19

Morty seemed to have forgotten the crucial rule about homeroom representatives; it made him persistent.

"I'd've thought you of all people would want to see Carla sweat a little."

"Carla doesn't sweat," I corrected. "She oozes Calvin Klein."

Morty laughed.

Lola said, "Well, of course I do . . ."

There was something in her voice that made me look at her. She was gazing somewhere above my head in that way she has, as though she's watching a movie being shown on the clouds. This is never a good sign. It means that she's thinking. Which in this case meant that she was about to come up with some outrageous scheme to circumvent the school constitution that would almost definitely involve me and wreak havoc with my stress levels. It was a good time to distract her.

"So, Morty," I said loudly and brightly. "Let's have that petition. I'll sign."

Lola stopped gazing at her private movie screen. She put her hand out to stop him. "Wait."

"Wait for what?" asked Morty. "I've got a pen right here."

Lola looked from him to me. Her eyes were glowing like something that was about to blow up.

"I just realized that I wasn't thinking laterally before. I was just thinking psychopathic mudslinging and having no time to reread *Lear* . . . But now I am thinking laterally. And I've got an idea!" She looked to me for encouragement, and when it didn't come, she went on without it. "You're right, Morty," Lola proclaimed, picking up steam and volume at the same time. "Carla can't be allowed to just swan into the presidency as if it's her birthright or something." She waved one of her scarves in the air. "She must be stopped!"

Someone behind me actually clapped.

Clapping, however, was not what I felt like doing. I stuffed my uneaten dessert back into my lunch box in what I hoped was a firm and significant manner. Lola is my best friend, but that doesn't make me blind to her faults. I'd known her long enough for the words "I've got an idea" to chill my heart.

"No," I said. "I don't want to know."

Lola looked wounded. "For God's sake, Ella . . . you haven't even heard what it is yet. You can't say no until you hear what it is."

"Yes, I can. And anyway, I have a pretty good idea what it is. You've found some way around the homeroom rep rule, haven't you?" Something devious.

Lola coyly tilted her head. "Well . . ."

"You just never know when to stop." I snapped my lunch box shut and grabbed the piece of paper from Morty's hands. "I'm signing Morty's petition," I said. "You're on your own on this one."

To my surprise, instead of arguing with me like she usually does, Lola just made a what-can-you-do kind of face and sighed like a doomed Greek heroine.

"Fine," she said. "I'll get the fifty signatures I need without your help."

"Good," I said. "You do that. But just remember one thing: There is no way I'm running with you for vice president. Is that totally and absolutely clear?"

"Don't get yourself all stirred up," answered Lola. "Running for vice president is the last thing on earth I'd want you to do."

How was I supposed to know she was telling the truth for a change?

4

My Mother and I Have a Conversation about the Election

There was a meeting of the school newspaper staff that afternoon.

Carla Santini had already bought a full-page ad for the next issue.

"Just so long as Carla understands that the paper is impartial," said Barry, our editor in chief. "We don't take sides."

"What sides?" asked one of the other reporters. "Morty Slinger's more a shadow than a side."

Everybody laughed.

"We may as well write up the election issue now," said someone else. "SANTINI BY A LANDSLIDE: YOU KNOW SHE'S THE BEST."

"Well, that's a little defeatist," I teased.

"And we're all a little defeated," said Barry. "Carla's got a better war record than the American army."

After the meeting we went for a pizza, so it was late by the time I got home.

My mother was on the sofa, watching something on TV and drinking a glass of wine. She always had a couple of glasses of wine in the evening, to help her relax. Lola wasn't the only one who wasn't quite sure what my mother was relaxing from.

"Hello, sweetheart," she called. "Have a good day?"

I said yes. Even if I'd had the worst day in the history of humankind, I probably wouldn't have told her. My mother doesn't handle disappointment well.

"Anything exciting happen?" asked my mother.

"No." I flopped down in one of the armchairs. "Not really."

My mother poured herself another glass. "I hear Carla's running for school president." She sounded pleased.

"Yeah," I said. "She is."

"You know," said my mother, "I was talking to Mela today . . ." Mela is Carmela Santini, mother of Carla.

I didn't want to get into a Carla Santini conversation with my mother, because a Carla Santini conversation always led to a Lola Cep one. My mother didn't like Lola. Lola isn't a character type my mother understands. My mother still had hopes then that I'd go back to hanging out with Carla Santini. Carla Santini she loved.

I stared hard at the television screen. "Really?"

I heard her put her glass down on the coffee table.

"Mela was saying that Carla's not very happy with Alma as her running mate . . ."

"No?"

I heard her pick her glass up again.

"As a matter of fact, Mela thinks that Carla would much rather have *you* run with her."

I nearly choked on my tongue. "You what?" I couldn't stop myself. I turned around. "You can't be serious."

My mother shrugged almost coyly. I wasn't sure if she was smiling again, or if she just hadn't stopped.

"I'm only telling you what Mela said."

What you have to understand is that this wasn't just idle conversation over coffee or the charity lunch. This was Carla Santini getting her mother to get my mother to convince me to run with her. That's the way our little community of Woodford works. The CIA could have taken lessons from this crew.

"Well, you can tell Mrs. Santini that I'm not interested."

"Oh, honey . . ." My mother rubbed a finger on the stem of her glass. "At least give it a little thought."

"I don't have to. I don't want to be vice president."

"But you and Carla used to be such good friends. Wouldn't it be nice to be doing something together again?"

Not unless I was guaranteed to come out alive.

"I'm really not interested in politics, Mom. I'm the shy and retiring type, remember?"

"But that's why you and Carla would make such a good team," said my mother. "And think of the victory party you could have if you and Carla won." Her voice rose with excitement. "We could have it here—it's been ages since we had a party—and I could do the catering . . ."

My mother was always catering for charity do's and her friends' parties and stuff like that. "Finger foods would be best—but not chips and dips. Chips and dips are sooo passé . . ."

"Mom, please . . . listen to me. I don't want to run for vice president. I really, really don't."

She looked into her glass. "And what about Lola?"

"What about her?"

She looked at me almost slyly. "Isn't she running? I can't imagine Lola missing an opportunity for attention like this."

I told you she didn't like Lola.

"Maybe," I said. "I'm not sure. But I'm not running with her."

"Really?"

"Really."

My mother gave me a curious look as she reached for the bottle.

"Well, I suppose that's something," said my mother.

5

Even the Most Mundane Election Can Hold a Surprise

I didn't tell Lola about my conversation with my mother. This was partly because I knew it would only wind her up; and partly because Lola spent the next few days being very involved in her new role of political agitator.

She was always busy. Too busy for lunch. Too busy to walk to class with me. Too busy to leave school when I did. She even cut us down to two phone calls a night, because she was so busy. The phone company must have thought she was ill.

"I've had a lot to do in a very short amount of time," Lola informed me on Wednesday. "The petitions have to be in by tomorrow afternoon."

I didn't want to encourage her—encouraging Lola is like encouraging dandelions, she just takes over—but I was pretty curious by then.

"So how's it going? No hitches?"

"Not one." She tapped the clipboard she now carried everywhere. "I shouldn't have any trouble meeting the quota."

"Really?" I didn't ask how she'd managed to get around the homeroom rep rule. I wanted to know, but I didn't want to become an accessory after the fact—the way I had when she "borrowed" Eliza Doolittle's dress from the drama department. "What about vice president? Who's that going to be?"

In only a few short days Lola had acquired a politician's smile. Possibly Hillary Clinton's.

"Sam."

"Sam?" She couldn't be serious. Sam Creek is not a person you associate with school politics. He's more a person you associate with revolution. "But he hasn't even been in school all week."

"Because he hurt his foot," explained Lola, as though Sam would never miss school unless he was practically dead. "Some car spare part rolled over it, or fell on it . . . something like that. Anyway, it doesn't matter. For a social deviant, Sam's a lot more popular than you'd think. It must be because most of the boys take their cars to him."

"Well," I said. "So everything's under control."

"Absolutely," said Lola.

I lowered my voice. "I do wish you luck, you know. It's not that I don't think you should be president. It's just that I don't want to see you get hurt."

Lola had been pretty upset when no one would believe that we'd been to the Sidhartha party and met the lead singer, Stu Wolff. It was the only time I'd seen her even temporarily defeated.

"I know that," said Lola. "Yours is a kind nature. But you don't have to worry, El. This time it's Carla Santini who's going to get hurt."

And then she dashed off to get some more signatures before the bell rang.

Carla Santini and her coven—Alma Vitters, Tina Cherry, and Marcia Conroy—were standing outside homeroom on Friday morning, the day the nominations were announced.

"There they are," muttered Lola. "The four cheerleaders of the apocalypse."

Carla Santini didn't look like a cheerleader today. She was wearing a tailored suit and a string of real pearls. She looked like an ambassador to the UN.

Carla was holding court as usual. She never once so much as glanced in our direction, but I knew she'd seen us coming down the hall. Her voice went up several decibels.

"I think Mork the Dork managed to get himself nominated," Carla boomed. "But aside from him, I don't think anyone else is running." She sounded as though this was a crushing disappointment. "So much for democratic institutions."

Tina Cherry shrieked, "Well, really, Carla. Who would run against you? You're everyone's first choice."

"And their only choice, apparently," said Lola.

She said it softly, but we were near enough to Carla and her crew that the Santini radar—imitated by bats, but never matched—could pick it up.

Carla purred, "I have to say, I was surprised to discover that you're not running, Lola."

She was going to be even more surprised when she discovered that Lola was.

Carla's smile darkened the corridor. "You're usually only too eager to humiliate yourself in public."

Lola put on her politician's grin. This time the politician was definitely Henry Kissinger.

"Oh, I'd much rather watch you humiliate yourself in public." She swung her shawl over her shoulder, making Carla jump back to avoid being hit. "And I have this very strong premonition that this just may be my chance."

"Mork the Dork?" Carla's laughter ricocheted down the hall, deadlier than a speeding bullet. "You think Morty Slinger is going to humiliate me? Most of the student body doesn't even know who he is. They think he works in the office."

"Every election has its surprises," said Lola. "Remember Truman? Remember Teddy Roosevelt?"

"Remember the Alamo," said Carla.

The nominations were the last announcement of the morning. Dr. Alsop did the honors. He started with his yearly lecture on the democratic process and the importance of participating in school government. And then, when even Carla Santini looked as if she might drop off, he cleared his throat.

"It gives me great pleasure to announce the nominations for the school elections," said Dr. Alsop. The PA crackled.

Carla looked up as though he'd called her name. Everyone else looked at Carla.

"For president," Dr. Alsop went on among more crackling, "Morton Slinger . . . Carla Santini . . ."

There was a burst of cheering and clapping from the Santini contingent that was so loud I nearly missed the third name.

". . . and Ella Gerard."

I might have convinced myself I'd misheard him if Sam, who had finally limped in to school, hadn't given a war whoop.

"Way to go, Ella!" shouted Sam.

Now, except for me, Lola, and Carla Santini, everybody was looking at me. Carla and I were looking at Lola. Lola was staring up at the PA as though this were all news to her.

Dr. Alsop was still going. "For vice president, Farley Brewbaker . . . Alma Vitters . . ."—another roar from Carla and her crew—"and Samuel Creek."

Mr. Geraldi, our homeroom teacher, laughed. "Good Lord, Sam," said Mr. Geraldi. "What'd you do? Lose a bet?"

Sam didn't shout out a war whoop this time. He leaned over Lola's shoulder. "Back up the truck here," hissed Sam. "What does he mean 'Samuel Creek'?"

Lola glanced back at him, rolling her eyes. "Well, Ella has to have a vice president, doesn't she?"

It was Carla who answered. Shakespeare warns about daggers in men's smiles, but her smile contained an intercontinental ballistic missile.

"What Ella's going to need is a pallbearer," said Carla Santini.

6

Yet More Conversations about the Election

God knows how she did it, but Carla Santini's face—larger than life and twice as scary—was plastered all over the school walls by the time we got out of homeroom.

"She must've hired elves," said Lola, as she, Sam, and I walked to our first class. "Look at this place. It looks like the Carla Santini Hall of Fame."

It was more like a Hall of Mirrors, but I didn't say so. I knew Lola's tricks. I was not going to be diverted from what I considered the primary topic of conversation that morning by a discussion on the speed and efficiency with which Carla had launched her campaign.

I gave her a cool look. "Personally, I'm a lot more interested in how you managed to get me and Sam nominated without us knowing."

"It was easy, really." Lola's smile was smug. She was pretty pleased with herself. "I just made sure I asked people who never talk to you. Which is at least half the school in your case, and almost all of it in Sam's."

"Well, you've really gone too far this time, Lola." It was stating the obvious, but I still felt it had to be said.

Sam agreed. "Way too far. Right off the road."

But the advantage of madness is that you're protected from anyone else's point of view.

"You're both overreacting." Lola's tone was matter-of-fact and breezy. "Once you have time to get used to the idea, you'll see that it's absolutely brilliant. Near genius."

Sam shook his head. "Get a grip on yourself, Einstein." His voice had more patience in it than you'd think a boy who looks like every mother's drug-crazed nightmare would possess. "Listen to me, Lola. I'm an anarchist. I can't run for vice president. I don't believe in government."

Lola's shawl flapped in his face. "Oh, please . . . How can you not believe in government? That's like not believing in air. And anyway, there's no better way to destroy an institution than from within."

Meet the girl with the answer for everything.

"Lola," I said. "Lola, you can't just go around nominating people without asking them first. It's not the way it's done."

She cocked an eyebrow in my direction. "Oh, really? Well, there's nothing in the rules that says you have to have the nominee's permission to put his or her name forward." She beamed. "I checked."

"That's because no one ever thought anyone would be dumb enough to do it," said Sam.

Lola carried on as though he hadn't spoken. "And besides, Ella . . ." She gave me one of her Melanie Griffith looks, innocent and misunderstood. "I know it was three days ago, but if you cast your mind back, you'll realize that I did try to tell you." She smiled sweetly. "But you didn't want to listen." She swung her arm for dramatic effect and whacked Sam in the nose. "In fact, you totally refused to listen."

"That's not true!"

"Oh, yes, it is." Lola surged forward, her shawl flapping behind her.

Sam and I trotted on either side of her, trying to keep up with her new power walk.

"Lola—" Even I could hear that I was bleating. "Lola, this is madness. Aside from the ethical issues, and the fact that neither of us wants to run, Sam and I don't stand a chance against Carla and Alma. Probably less than Morty."

"Oh, please . . ." Lola sighed. "You have much more of a chance than Morty." She lowered her voice to a whisper. "Morty's a nice guy, but he's so dull."

"And I'm not?"

Carla Santini dumped me when we started high school because I was so dull she didn't want to be associated with me.

"No," said Lola, "you're not. You're like a bomb that's only waiting to be detonated to light the night with a thousand flames."

I have no idea where she gets this stuff from.

35

"Tell us the truth, Lola," said Sam. "What planet do you really come from?"

I bleated some more. "Lola, listen to me. I'm not going to light the night with anything except an electric bulb. I can't do this, Lola. It'll kill me. I'm introverted, remember? Underneath my name in the yearbook it's going to say *'Shy to those who don't know her, Ella's sense of humor is loved by the few who know her well. . . .'* I am not presidential material."

"Yes, you are." She grabbed my shoulders as though she were going to shake me. "You can do it. You're exactly what's needed. You're smart, you're well liked, your ego doesn't dominate your personality, you're as honest and trustworthy as Bill Gates is rich, and you were a homeroom rep your first year." She winked. "Plus, you're perfect. There's not the teensiest little thing in your life or your past that even a professional character assassin like Carla Santini could use against you."

Sam groaned. "It's even worse when she starts making sense," he said to me. "It makes me really nervous."

It made me pretty nervous, too.

"But that's not the point, Lola. The point is that I do not want to run." I said the second sentence very slowly, enunciating every letter. I might as well have said it in Greek.

Lola gazed into my eyes, sincerely and with just a hint of disappointment. "But the people need you."

"A few days ago it was *you* they needed," I reminded her.

Lola didn't find this an obstacle. "But they can't have me, so now they need *you*." She tightened her grip on my shoulders. "You can't turn your back on the people, Ella. They nominated you. They want you to run." She looked to Sam. "And you. You're both the people's choice."

"Lola," I begged, "give us a break, will you? Even if we were the people's choice, we'd still have to campaign. Neither Sam nor I know anything about running a political campaign."

"Well, that's where you're in luck, isn't it?" Lola beamed. "You've got the hottest campaign manager in the state on your team."

"I take it we're talking about Lola Cep," I said.

"You can't lose," Lola assured me. "I may have a thespian soul, but my mind is pure Machiavelli."

"What's Machiavelli?" asked Sam.

"And that's another thing," Lola informed him. "You're going to have to improve your school attendance if you want to be vice president, Sam. It's best to lead by example."

"But I don't want to be vice president," snarled Sam. "I didn't choose this."

"Sometimes," said Lola, "we can't do what we choose. Sometimes we have to do what we must."

"I'm beginning to feel like I must kill you," Sam muttered.

But Lola didn't hear him. She was already halfway to her desk.

7

Dr. Alsop Gets in on the Conversation
and More or Less Ends It

Since Lola wouldn't accept the fact that we weren't going to run, Sam and I decided that as soon as lunch period started, we'd go to see Dr. Alsop and respectfully decline the nomination in an adult, responsible way. It seemed pretty straightforward and easy as plans go. I was outside Sam's computer class just after the bell rang. It took ages for him to come out because there was a girl in the year below us handing out glossy "Vote for Carla Santini" fliers at the door. No one got out without one.

Sam was crumpling his into a ball as he stepped into the hall. He started to smile, but then his eyes saw something behind me and he stopped. "What the hell is that?"

I didn't look around. I'd already seen it. "It's a poster. There seem to be quite a few around the school." I laughed grimly. "Lola really has been working hard."

"'Gerard and Creek,'" read Sam. "'Real People for a Real Choice.'" He was shaking his head in a disbelieving kind of way. "That should appeal to Carla's sense of humor. What's Lola trying to do, start a war?"

"What do you mean *start*?" The private war between Lola Cep and Carla Santini had been going on from almost the moment they met. They were the Montagues and Capulets of Dellwood High, and neither was likely to ever put down her weapon.

Sam was still shaking his head. "But how does she work so fast? Do you think it's prescription drugs?"

"No. It's demonic possession."

Sam laughed. "No, really."

"Really."

"She sure is something, isn't she?" Now he was laughing and shaking his head. "She's got more balls than a pool hall. Without a word to anyone, she's organized the whole shebang."

"Oh, don't tell me you're weakening," I blurted out. There was definitely a hint of abject pleading in my voice. Without Sam's support, I would be a lump of wet clay in Lola's hands, and I knew it. Lola knew it, too.

"No way!" Sam gave me a surprised look. "Of course I'm not weakening. My mother didn't raise any pushovers, you know. Nobody railroads me into anything, not even Lola."

I wasn't completely convinced. "Well," I said. I cleared my throat. "You did borrow Eliza's—"

"She *asked* me to borrow the dress," cut in Sam. "She gave me a choice." He grinned. "And anyway, it was a totally different situation."

"You mean this one is legal."

"No, I mean I was backstage. I'm not a spotlight kind of guy."

Which made two of us. I'm not a spotlight kind of girl, either; I'm a sitting-in-the-middle-of-the-theater-where-it's-dark-but-you-can-see-what's-happening kind of girl.

Sam grabbed my elbow and started steering me down the hall. "Come on. We'd better find Old Gumshoes before he goes to lunch."

Dr. Alasdair Alsop, or Old Gumshoes as Sam called him, was in the main office, talking to Mrs. Baggoli.

They both looked up as Sam and I came through the door.

"Speak of the devils!" cried Dr. Alsop. "Ella! Sam! I'm so glad to see you! Mrs. Baggoli and I were just talking about you."

"It's an alien takeover," whispered Sam. "He's *never* glad to see me."

I'd been concentrating so hard on what I was going to say to Dr. Alsop that now that he was standing in front of me, I couldn't speak. I smiled.

Sam said, "Dr. Alsop, Ella and I wondered if we could talk to you."

Dr. Alsop laughed. Maybe it was an alien takeover. I didn't know Dr. Alsop as well as Sam did, since I'd never been sent to his office in my life, but I knew him well enough to know that he didn't exactly have a reputation for laughing too much.

"Now that makes a change, doesn't it?" boomed Dr. Alsop. "*You* wanting to talk to *me!*"

Mrs. Baggoli, Ms. Littlemoon—Dr. Alsop's secretary—and the handful of students waiting at the front desk all joined in the laughter.

Sam sort of grunted a couple of times. "Yeah," he said, "I guess it is." He kicked me in the shin.

I forced myself to say something. "It'll only take a couple of minutes, Dr. Alsop. I mean, if you don't have the time, we could always come—"

"Time?" roared Dr. Alsop. "Of course I have time for you two. To tell you the truth, I'm delighted you stopped by. I was hoping to have a chance to congratulate you personally."

Sam was obviously as thrown by this as I was. "Congratulate us about what?" he asked.

Everybody laughed again, but no one laughed louder than Dr. Alsop.

When he finally chuckled to a stop, he said, "It's always good to have someone with a sense of humor in a political race. Sharpens things up."

Sam and I said, "Oh," but neither of us had a chance to say more than that because Mrs. Baggoli suddenly joined the conversation.

"I'm sure you have a lot to discuss with Dr. Alsop," said Mrs. Baggoli. "But before I go, let me congratulate you on your nominations, too." While she was talking, she started moving away from Dr. Alsop. I willed her to keep walking until she was back in the hallway, but she stopped next to Sam and me. She lowered her voice. "Between you and me, I think this is just what the election needs. Fresh blood."

Fresh blood all over the campus was what she meant. My blood and Sam's.

Mrs. Baggoli grabbed my hand and shook it vigorously. "Congratulations, Ella. It's really good to see you using some of your potential."

My potential for disaster, obviously.

I managed to smile. "Thank you, Mrs. Baggoli."

"And as for you, Sam Creek." She then took Sam's hand. "I've been waiting for this day for a long, long time."

I could hear Sam swallow. "Yeah," he mumbled. "Me, too."

All of a sudden, Dr. Alsop was standing next to us. "I couldn't agree more with Mrs. Baggoli. We're all very proud of Carla Santini, of course. She's always been a credit to this school—but it's nice to see someone else getting into the middle of things for a change. Especially you two."

Sam did some vague grunting and I kept smiling. I couldn't believe this was happening.

"I truly welcome your nominations," finished Dr. Alsop. He extended his hand to me. "I've always had the feeling that you tend to hide your light under a bushel, Ella. This has come as a most welcome surprise."

What I wanted to hide under a bushel right then was me.

I couldn't tell him I was backing out now; I just couldn't. He looked so happy. And there were so many witnesses.

I glanced over at Sam. He looked like he'd swallowed a spark plug. He wasn't going to say anything, either.

I reached for Dr. Alsop's hand. "Thank you," I said.

Then Dr. Alsop shook Sam's hand. "And as for you, Mr. Creek, surprise doesn't begin to describe how I feel. It's very gratifying that you've made this decision. I think we've really turned a corner here."

"Yeah," Sam mumbled in my ear. "Right into a wall."

8

Carla Santini Changes My Mind

I always went over to Lola's after school on Friday after-noons. Friday was Lola's sisters-sitting day and she couldn't come to me, and it was also my mother's after-noon as a volunteer at the local nursing home, so she didn't get home till late. And since I was going to Lola's and Sam had to work, I was the one who was volun-teered to explain Sam's and my position on the election to Lola. Which was that, having failed to resign, we would be in the election but not really part of it. We would be candidates in name only.

Lola and I stopped in town to pick up the badges she'd ordered on the way home.

She talked all the way. Blah-blah-blah the election . . . the election blah-blah-blah. She didn't notice that I was quiet and pensive. I was waiting for the right moment to give her a shot of reality.

The badges were kind of black and a shade of yellow I associate with the flu. The writing was fuzzy.

"They're the cheapest I could get," said Lola. "We don't exactly have a big budget."

We had a total budget of $150 from the school fund. Each of the candidates got that.

"We'll need some money to buy paper for more posters and stuff like that," said Lola as we pedaled to her house. "But we won't need any money for the actual production." Besides the cash, on Monday each candidate would be given an empty room to use after classes as his or her headquarters, a key to the photocopy machine in the office, and use of a computer. "The graphics program the art department has is excellent."

I said, "Um," which was basically what I'd been saying since we left school.

"We'll have to have a rally, of course, so you can give your major speech. But we can use the gym, so that won't cost anything."

This really cheered me up; incredible as it may seem, I'd forgotten about the speech giving.

"Great," I said. Major as in "big" was bad enough; major as in "more than one" was my worst nightmare come true. The one time we had to give a speech in English, I was so nervous that I threw up my breakfast. I had to run out of homeroom with my hand over my mouth. When I actually got up to speak, I was shaking so much it sounded like I was playing maracas, not discussing the symbolism of William Blake. "Terrific."

"So that puts us way ahead," continued Lola. "We can use the money for something really spectacular . . ." She gazed at the road ahead for a few minutes with the glazed eyes of someone having a vision, and then glanced at me. "How much do you think a hot air balloon would cost?"

"More than a hundred and fifty."

"I wonder . . . ," said Lola.

All the way to her house she tried to think of something spectacular we could do for less than $150. What about skywriting? What about hiring a marching band? What about mimes? What about a short film? What about Sam and me jumping from a plane with a banner that said MAKE THE LEAP?

"Will you get a grip on yourself?" I asked as we finally shut the door of her room behind us. "I know I speak for Sam when I say that nobody is jumping out of a plane. Not even a small one. Not even one you've talked some poor chump into letting us use for free."

Lola looked at me as if I were being unreasonable. "You know, you could show a little more enthusiasm, El." She put the snack tray on the bed and sat down beside it. "Enthusiasm is a very important factor in any campaign. Especially among the candidates."

I picked up a grape, but I didn't feel like eating it; I felt like throwing it at her. And that's when I told her.

"You know," I said, "you really are too much. Not only do you get me and Sam into this without so much as a word, but you then expect us to be enthusiastic." I squashed the grape between my fingers. "Well, we're not enthusiastic, Lola. We'll run because we can't get out of running, but that's as far as it goes. Enthusiasm is not included."

46

"You mean that you'll walk, but not run," said Lola. She popped a grape into her mouth. "You'll go through the motions, but really you're just handing the election to Carla Santini on a silver platter. Neither of you cares what happens."

"Exactly," I said. "You finally understand. You can drag a horse to water, but you can't make it drink."

Lola popped another grape into her mouth. "I'm surprised at you, Ella." She chewed slowly. "Really surprised. I thought you enjoyed a good fight."

"No, you didn't." Lola's voice was calm and quiet, but mine was loud and shrill. "*You* enjoy a good fight. I never fight with anyone, and you know it."

"You fight with me all the time," said Lola. "You're fighting with me now."

"That's besides the point. You don't understand what it's like to be me, Lola." Against my will, my voice started shaking. "I really am shy and retiring. I've always been shy and retiring. The only thing I could run for president of would be a club of one."

She swung a tiny bunch of grapes in the air. "Oh, please . . . you're getting yourself all worked up over nothing as usual. You're one of the most logical, intelligent, and competent teenagers I know. You're going to be brilliant. This is going to be your golden hour."

"No, it isn't," I snapped. "If you have your way, it's going to be one of those black and humiliating hours. You're overestimating me. I can't do it. I'll pretend that I'm doing it, but that's all. You can't expect more than that."

47

Lola dropped her grapes and grabbed my shoulders. "But you can do it, Ella. I have faith in you. I know you can rise to the occasion."

"No, I can't." My voice screeched, more or less imploring. "Lola, I can't go around smiling and shaking hands with people I don't even know. I can't meet Carla and Morty in a debate. I can't stand up in front of the student body and give a speech."

"Why not?"

My voice screeched some more. "Because I'm shy and retiring."

"No, you're not," said Lola. "What you are is a victim of your own dubious self-image." She gave me a look. I know she blames my parents for this. She thinks they've tried to smother me. "You *think* you're shy and retiring, therefore you are. All you've got to do is change the way you think."

"No, you have to change the way *you* think." I threw the grape I'd been holding back in the bowl. "Sam and I are agreed: we keep our names in the race, but we do no more than the barest minimum."

"And that's your final word?" asked Lola.

"Yes," I said. "That's my final word."

My mother was in the kitchen when I got home. There were several opened cookbooks, a notebook, and a glass of wine on the table in front of her.

She looked up as I came through the door. "There you are! Where have you been? I was getting worried."

48

"Didn't you get my message?" I gave her a kiss on the cheek. "I left one on your cell phone."

My mother blinked. "Oh, your message . . . yes . . . of course . . ." Even her smile seemed to be blinking.

"Have a good day?"

"Yes," said my mother. "Well . . ." She continued to blink and smile. It was really eerie. "Mrs. Mopper passed away this morning." Mrs. Mopper was my mother's favorite old lady in the nursing home. They both went to Sarah Lawrence, they both married lawyers, and they both had one child and liked golf and bridge and gourmet cooking.

"Gee . . . ," I stammered, " . . . I'm sorry. I—"

"I know . . . I know . . . ," chanted my mother. "But she was very old . . ." I could hear her take a deep breath. "Anyway, when I got home, I got so involved with the menu for the arthritis lunch that I forgot all about your message."

I didn't know what to say now. I hadn't gotten past Mrs. Mopper yet. I said, "Oh."

My mother was still blinking and smiling. "I just didn't think you'd be so late." She laughed. It sounded as if she were gargling. "It's your father who's always late. Not you. Your father's always late."

"Dad's not home yet?" I kept my voice light and casual; as if I thought my father might be home, or that it wasn't unusual that he wasn't.

"Work, of course." She picked up her glass and downed it in one. "Work, work, work, work, work. You'd think he was one of the Seven Dwarfs."

It didn't seem like a good time to tell her about the election. It would only set her off. Most of the time my mother was totally normal, but sometimes instead of a couple of glasses of wine in the evening, she had a couple of bottles. And when she did, instead of getting all happy and dancing around with a lampshade on her head like you're supposed to, she got depressed. The mention of my father always working was a sign that the lampshades were safe.

"Have you eaten?" I asked. "You want me to stick something in the microwave for you?"

My mother's eyes widened in mock horror. "But what about your father? You don't want him to eat alone, do you?"

"What about a snack?" I suggested. "I could fix you a bagel with grilled cheese." My mother can cook any food from French to Thai, but I stop pretty much at irradiated cheese.

She was already getting up, however, holding her glass the way the Statue of Liberty holds her torch, only not as steadily.

"What I want is more wine," she announced. "That's what I want."

I watched her go over to the refrigerator. She was starting to wobble. "Cheese goes well with wine," I said.

My mother wasn't listening. She was yanking a bottle out of the fridge.

"I want you to promise me something, honey," said

my mother. "Don't you become a workaholic like your father. It's important to have some fun, as well."

"I know," I said. "I do."

She shook the corkscrew at me. "Fun is very important. You cannot live by bread alone."

Or by white wine, I thought, watching the corkscrew.

"You don't know how fast your life slips away," my mother went on. "You think you have forever . . . You think there's always more time . . ."

I sort of stopped listening. I'd heard this all before— and I didn't really want to hear it again. It was one of my mother's monologues that could end in tears.

I was trying to ease my way out of the kitchen when I was literally saved by the bell. The phone rang.

"I'll get it!" I shouted.

I'd just lifted the receiver when my mother, suddenly happy, said, "That'll be Carla. She's been calling you all night. I think she wants to invite you to a party."

"Hi, Ella." Carla's voice bubbled through the phone like a chemistry experiment that requires a mask and gloves. "How's it going?"

She sounded as though calling me to chat on a Friday night was a regular occurrence. About as regular as a blue moon.

The cork popped. "Is that Carla?" asked my mother.

I nodded. "Fine," I said into the receiver. "And you?"

Carla's laugh was as delicate as a surgical knife. "I can't complain. I'm really looking forward to the summer. My mother's taking me to Europe. Daddy feels a Continental experience will help me get into Harvard."

As though she needed help. Mr. Santini was rich enough to be one of Harvard's favorite alumni.

"Wow," I said. "That sounds terrific."

My mother's voice shot across the kitchen. "Is it a party, Ella? Is she inviting you to a party?" I clapped my hand over the mouthpiece.

Carla gushed on, explaining just how terrific a Continental experience was going to be. I stared at the clock on the microwave and waited for her to finish and tell me why she'd called. It took four and a half minutes.

Carla finished off Spain and all it had to offer, and then she said, "Gloriana!" as though she'd been goosed or something. She giggled. "Listen to me talk about *me* . . ."

Now *that* was unusual.

". . . When the reason I called was to talk about *you!*"

I swear the earth stood still.

"Me?"

"Of course, *you!*" Carla giggled some more.

From behind me and well into her second bottle of chardonnay, my mother hissed, "Tell her you'll go, Ella. Have some fun."

I was holding the mouthpiece so tightly that my hand hurt.

"You know how much I've always liked and admired you," Carla was saying. "I've always considered you a very solid person, Ella. Reliable . . . trustworthy . . ."

Like a Girl Scout.

I braced myself.

"And we have been friends practically from birth . . ."

She was definitely about to go for a major artery.

"That's why I was thinking how perfect it would be if you ran as my vice presidential candidate. Santini and Gerard—together again."

Here, ladies and gentlemen, is a girl who absolutely never gives up. You can see why Carla and Lola are mortal enemies. The state of New Jersey isn't really big enough for the both of them.

"Excuse me?"

"It just seems so silly for you to run *against* me, when we'd make such a dynamite team. You know, glamour *and* ordi— normality, all on one ticket."

No points for guessing which I was.

"Tell her yes!" my mother called again. The bottle clinked against her glass. "You don't go out enough."

I was practically pressing myself into the wall. "What happened to Alma? I thought she was running with you."

"Oh, Alma!" Carla sighed. "You know what Alma's like. She's a little frivolous for something as serious as this."

"But she's already been nominated."

"That's just a technicality. It can be changed."

Thus spoke a natural politician. In Carla's world, there is nothing that can't be changed if she wants it changed.

I cleared my throat. "Well," I said, "I don't know what to say. You've taken me by surprise."

"Say yes!" cried my mother. "Say you'll go."

"Is that a yes?" asked Carla.

One of the things I never missed after Carla Santini and I went our separate ways was being her trusty side-kick, the original yes-girl.

"Well, no," I said, lowering my voice. "I'm really sorry, Carla, but I can't change my mind about running for president now. Dr. Alsop—"

"Dr. Alsop?" Carla's shriek turned into laughter. "Still the same old Ella, always worried about what other people will say . . ."

I said, "But—"

Carla said, "Never mind Dr. Alsop. He's just a technicality, too."

Harvard wasn't the only school that benefited from Mr. Santini's generosity.

My mother's voice was still humming in the background: *We could go shopping . . . get something special . . . have lunch somewhere nice . . . Wouldn't it be fun . . .*"

I lowered my own voice even more. "I'm sorry, Carla, but I really can't."

"You're sure?"

"Yes, I'm sure."

There was a moment in which all I could hear was my mother saying, "Oh, don't say no, darling . . . Have some fun . . ."—and the Santini artillery clunking into place.

And then Carla said, "I hope you realize what you're doing, Ella. I really don't advise this. It would be better for everybody if you came over to me."

I stared at the receiver. Her voice had lost its girlish warmth.

"All I'm doing is keeping my word."

"No," corrected Carla. "You're doing more than that."

"Is this another death threat?"

Carla laughed. "I'm not trying to kill you, Ella. I'm trying to save you from public suicide. This is going to be a no-holds-barred campaign. And, personally, I don't think you're up to it. I think this could demolish you."

I was still staring at the phone. I don't usually get *really* angry, but I was getting really angry now. I wasn't even friends with Carla anymore, and she thought that I'd do what she wanted.

"Come on, honey," crooned my mother. "Tell Carla you'll go . . ."

"I'm your friend, Ella. I'm trying to do you a favor," Carla was saying. I was amazed she even knew what a favor was. "You should be smart enough to take it."

It was as if all the times in the last sixteen years when I should have gotten mad and stood up for myself—and not just with Carla Santini—had stuffed themselves into this moment. What happened to all my potential? What happened to all the light I was hiding under a bushel? What happened to Lola's sincere belief that I could rise to the occasion? In the world of Carla Santini none of these things existed. Yet.

"Well, here's a first," I said. "For once in your life you're wrong. I'm not going to take it."

"You used to be smart—before you started hanging out with riffraff." I could hear Carla smile. "Or does Lola have such power over you that you can't even say no to her when it's in your best interests?"

"Here's another first," I said.

I hung up the phone.

9

I Decide to Tell My Mother My Big News

Nothing happened after I hung up the phone on Carla. The oak beams of the kitchen floor didn't open and swallow me whole; a bolt of lightning didn't hit the house; the world didn't come to an untimely end. I stood there for a couple of seconds—waiting—but aside from my mother knocking over the wine bottle, nothing moved. I couldn't believe it.

I'd never hung up the phone on anyone before. It wasn't the way I was raised. If my mother had realized what I'd done, she would have blamed the bad influence of Lola Cep and made me call Carla back to apologize. But I didn't feel the tiniest desire to apologize. I didn't feel guilty at all. I felt like those people you see on TV who take a three-day course in self-assertiveness and change their lives. And all I did was hang up the phone. I should have done it in first grade. I felt great.

I'm not saying that slamming the receiver down on Carla Santini made me think I could win the election, but it definitely made me feel like fighting. I mean, looking at it objectively, I had nothing to lose. At the very least I could have some fun annoying Carla. That wouldn't exactly make my mother happy, but it would cheer up everyone else.

I woke up on Saturday morning intending to tell my parents about the election at breakfast. Since my father isn't Mela Santini's best friend, I figured if I did it when he and my mother were together, he would be a balancing influence on her. Stop her from going into cardiac arrest.

My mother was in the kitchen when I went down. She was in a good mood. She moved around the room like a skater, gliding from the stove to the counter and the counter to the table, whisking the eggs and stirring the potatoes and sniffing the air to see if her rolls were done, singing to herself all the while. If she could remember anything about being so drunk the night before, she'd decided not to mention it. All she talked about was Mrs. Mopper. My mother was going to help Mrs. Mopper's daughter sort out her things that afternoon.

While my mother talked, I thought about what I was going to say when my father joined us. *Hey, guess what? I've got great news . . . Oh, did I tell you? I'm running for school president . . .* Stuff like that.

I think my mother must have forgotten about my father, because she jumped when he finally burst into the room calling, "Good morning, darling! How are my girls?"

"Darling!" My mother laughed. "You gave me a fright. I didn't hear you coming down the hall."

My parents always called each other darling. When I was little I thought that was their names: Darling Gerard and Darling Gerard. Lola called them the Darlings.

He winked at me and gave her a peck on the cheek. "Something smells good," said my father.

My mother beamed. "Sautéed potatoes and home-made rolls." She pushed back her chair. "What kind of omelet do you want?"

"No time." He hurled himself toward the coffeemaker. "Tony just called. He's already at the club."

Tony is Anthony P. Santini, golf aficionado and father of Carla—and a man who, if you ask me, has a lot to answer for.

My mother kept smiling. "But, darling . . . It'll only take a few min—"

"Really." My father snapped the lid on the insulated cup he uses in the car. "I've got a hell of a day. Not a minute to breathe."

My mother said, "Oh."

"Tell you what, though," he went on. "Tomorrow we'll all do something together. How does that sound? Take a drive. Have lunch somewhere nice . . ."

"What about tonight?" My mother was still smiling, but only with her mouth.

My father didn't know what time he'd get home. He had an afternoon meeting; he was having dinner with a client in New York. He gave her another peck on the cheek, winked in my direction again, and left.

My mother watched the doorway for a few seconds, and then she turned back to me. "Well," she said. She picked up her coffee cup. "And what are your plans for today?"

My plans for today were to go over to Lola's. Sam's father lets him off work at four on Saturdays, so we were having our first campaign meeting then. All I had to tell my mother, of course, was that I was going to Lola's, but instead I told her the whole thing. I figured the election would be over if I waited for my father.

Much to my surprise, my mother's first reaction was to clap. "But, sweetheart . . . That's wonderful. I'm so happy—you decided to run with Carla after all."

I should have known.

"No," I said quickly, "you've misunderstood me." I scooped the last of my omelet onto some toast. "I'm not running with Carla—I'm running *against* her."

This information noticeably decreased her happiness. "You're doing what?"

I ducked behind my juice glass. "I'm running against Carla. For president."

"But, sweetheart," said my mother, "Carla's . . . Carla's so popular . . . Do you really think you can win?"

"Well . . ." I smiled in what I hoped was a positive way. "One can but try, right?"

"I must say," said my mother, her eyes on the coffee in her cup, "that I'm a little surprised Lola is willing to accept vice president. That isn't like her at all." My mother's Lola smile is thin and wry. "You know . . . bride at the wedding . . . corpse at the funeral . . ."

"Campaign manager at the election," I filled in. "It's Sam who's running with me, not Lola."

"Who?"

"Sam—Sam Creek. You remember. The boy who sat with us at the school play?"

Her eyelids twitched. She did remember. She'd just found someone that she liked even less than she liked Lola Cep.

"Oh, Ella! Honey . . . Think what you're doing . . . Who's going to vote for a boy like that?"

I pushed my plate away. It was a good question. And I had a good answer. "Hopefully the same people who vote for me."

10

Viva la Revolución

Lola couldn't have been happier about Carla's call and my new mood of commitment to the fight. Despite Marilyn Gerard's misgivings about my chances, Lola said that Carla calling me like that proved I was a real threat to her. I was an immovable force. I was an unsurpassable obstacle. I had her on the run.

"Now all we have to do is secure our advantage," said Lola.

"You mean like have Carla kidnapped?" asked Sam. He'd arrived straight from work with grease under his nails and a significant amount of attitude.

"It would only backfire," said Lola. "She'd win on the sympathy vote. No, we need something that won't get us arrested."

"Yeah, right," said Sam. "But there is one little problem with that."

Lola frowned. "Which is . . . ?"

"Which is that anything we can do, Carla can do bigger and better. Carla's got more money than El Salvador and the crowd appeal of potato chips. If we spent every dime we had on a billboard in the middle of the court-yard, Carla would put her name up in neon lights."

I kept remembering what my mother said: *Carla's so popular . . . Carla's so popular . . .* Popularity was something I knew all about. Hard though it may be to believe, I used to be popular, too. When I was friends with Carla Santini. But as soon as she dumped me, I automatically became less popular than tooth decay. Popularity, it seemed to me, is both fickle and pointless.

"You know what I think?" I said. "I think we need to make sure that the election isn't about popularity. Unless we do that, we don't have even the smallest chance."

Lola looked back at me like a proud parent. "Didn't I tell you you'd rise to the occasion? That's absolutely brilliant, El. I think you've found the key."

I wasn't so sure about its being brilliant. It seemed to me that I was reaching for the thinnest straw more than I was rising, but at least it was a start.

Though possibly not much of one.

"And how are we going to do that?" Sam stretched out on the floor, leaning back on his elbows. "It may have escaped your notice, ladies, but as far as Carla's concerned, the only issues in this election are whether or not the cheerleaders are getting new uniforms or if the school trip's going to be to Williamsburg or Greece."

"But that's what Ella's saying," argued Lola. "Our platform has to represent emotional and spiritual growth for the student body of Dellwood High. We have to offer a new present and a brighter tomorrow!"

"You mean like Morty Slinger campaigning for more vegetarian food in the cafeteria?" asked Sam.

Lola slowly shook her head. "I don't consider that a vote getter. If it were, you could bet your last tube of lip gloss that Carla would be using it. No . . ." She raised her arms and spread them in the air. "We need something bigger. Something that transcends the ordinary and petty concerns of high school life."

I'm more a linear than a lateral thinker. "You mean like organic food versus genetically modified food? Stuff like that?"

Lola gazed back at me unblinking. "What?"

"What I mean is instead of just coming out for more vegetarian options in the cafeteria like Morty, we take a stand on genetic engineering. You know, the large issue that transcends the ordinary and petty concerns of high school life."

"I like it." Lola sat up straight. "I think you're heading in the right direction. If we're going to make this a contest that's about more than skirt lengths and how much money we spend on the Homecoming dance, then that's the kind of thing we're talking about." She raised her chin, her Joan of Arc–at-the-stake look in her eyes. "A vote has to mean more than being invited to Carla's next party."

Sam was shaking his head. "Yeah, yeah . . . That's just dandy. But you still haven't said how you plan to do that."

She gave him a pitying look; Saint Joan being forced to explain the voices.

"By making the students of Dellwood High realize that they're part of a larger world—that there are things that really matter."

Sam laughed. "Our platform's going to be to involve the school in world affairs? What are we going to do?"

Lola was scowling. "Ella just told you what we're going to do—we're going to do things like support non-genetically modified food—"

"And recycling," I added. "And the environment."

Lola nodded. "And homelessness and illiteracy—" She sat up, her arms raised in the air. "I can see it! It's just like John F. Kennedy."

"It sounds more like Che Guevara," said Sam.

She gave him one of the scornful looks she usually reserves for people who don't like Shakespeare.

"Oh, how quickly they forget," said Lola. She got to her feet, her hands on an imaginary dais. "'Ask not what your country can do for you,'" Lola intoned. "'Ask what you can do for your country!'"

Sam yawned. "Well, *that* should cause a revolution."

Lola scowled. "Stop being so negative," she ordered. "Everything Carla does is no more than a cheap attempt to buy votes. She's shallow and frivolous, and everything she stands for is shallow and frivolous, too. We don't want to be like her. We're the party of serious choice. We offer meaningful debate, not glamour and popularity."

"Which would be great if the students of Dellwood High preferred meaningful debate to glamour and popularity," said Sam.

II

Dellwood High Joins the Third World

Sam gave us a lift to school on Monday morning, more because Lola made him than because he wanted to.

Lola and I spent most of Sunday designing a new poster and trying to come up with appropriate slogans for the campaign, but Sam had refused another meeting. Sunday was his one day off, and he wasn't going to spend it trying to start a car without an engine, as he put it. Lola had looked like she wanted to remove his engine when he told her, but this morning she was being more philosophical. In fact, we were both in a pretty positive mood. Sam, however, was not.

"'Be a Part of Your World, Not a Part of Its Problems'?" He laughed. "Isn't that a little too much like that line from the sixties: 'If you're not part of the solution, you're part of the problem'?"

Lola grabbed hold of the door as we took the turn into the school drive a little sharply, but her eyes were on Sam. This was the third of our slogans he'd rejected.

"Well, what about this one, then? This one's Ella's: 'It's Time to Give Instead of Receive.'"

Sam glanced back at me in the rearview mirror. "No offense, Ella, but it sounds like a greeting card. If you want to put them to sleep, you might as well hypnotize them. Then at least we'd have a chance of getting them to vote for us."

"You're absolutely determined to be a thorn in our side rather than a spur on our boot, aren't you?" snapped Lola.

"I'm just saying what I think," said Sam.

"Well, I think you're wrong," said Lola. "I like it. It's simple but dramatic."

"You're simple but dramatic." We lurched to a stop in front of the school. "You guys get out here. I'll catch up with you after I've parked."

Lola and I were still talking about giving as opposed to receiving by the time we reached the school grounds. It was immediately pretty clear just who was giving what and who was receiving it.

In front of us was the courtyard. There were a lot of students in the courtyard, but there was a lot of something else, too: posters. All the posters that Carla had up on Friday had been taken down and replaced with new ones. They were on the walls; they were on the trees; they were on the trash cans; there were even two on the bike rack. The new posters featured the same professional photograph of Carla as their predecessors, but with two attention-grabbing additions. Each poster was framed in blue and silver stars, and each contained the message VOTE FOR SANTINI—DON'T LET IT BE SAID

THAT JUST ANYBODY CAN BE PRESIDENT OF DELLWOOD
HIGH.

"Ye gods!" cried Lola. "The Santini elves certainly
have been busy."

"Busy? She must be giving them drugs."

It didn't look to me like Carla was working to budget.
Not our budget. The Pentagon's maybe, but definitely
not ours.

I scanned the courtyard from left to right. "I only see a
couple of Slinger posters."

"That's a couple more than I see of Gerard-Creek,"
said Lola.

I could feel my heart miss a beat. "Oh, she couldn't
have." My eyes darted from wall to tree to trash can,
looking for our names in the forest of the Smiling Santini. "Not even Carla—I mean, I don't know much about
politics, but surely there must be a couple of rules."

"Only one," said Lola tersely. "Don't get caught." Her
book bag thumped over her shoulder. "Come on," she
ordered. "We're not standing for this!"

"Where are we going?"

"Where do you think? We're going to confront the
lion in her den." She pointed to the windows of the student common room. "Or, in this case, the weasel."

The common room was packed and noisy. We had no
trouble finding Carla in the mob, though. As usual, she
was sitting in the middle of the largest group (if Carla
were a celestial body and not a teenage girl, she'd be the

sun), flanked by Alma Vitters, Tina Cherry, and Marcia Conroy, but it was the cloud of blue and silver balloons over her head that really gave her away.

Carla was busy smiling like a salesman on commission and telling people to vote for her, but she looked up the second Lola and I stepped through the door. You might almost have thought she'd been waiting for us.

Lola marched across the room as though the words "determined" and "grimly" were in her stage directions.

"Why, Lola . . . Ella . . ." The only things I've ever heard that purr like Carla Santini are Rolls-Royce engines and very big cats, though by the way the group in front of her immediately parted, hers might have been the voice of the Lord. "Have you come to wish me luck?" She picked up a badge from the box in front of her and held it toward us. "Or did you want one of these?"

Carla's badges were a very attractive silver and blue, and besides being in focus, her name actually lit up and blinked.

The sight of the badge distracted Lola from her mission. She stared at the flashing name for a couple of seconds, and then looked back at Carla. "What is that? You're not going to try to convince us that you're paying for this stuff with the money from the school?"

Carla is good at looking innocent, too. "There's nothing in the rules that says you can't use private funds as well."

Lola and I said, "But it's not fair," together.

"'Fair'?" twittered Carla. "Of course it's fair. This is a democracy, remember? You two *do* believe in democracy, don't you?"

She was going to be telling everyone we were fascists next.

"Of course we do," I answered loudly. "But it doesn't seem very democratic to me that a person can win an election just because she has more money than her opponents."

"And where does stealing the other side's posters fit into this democracy of yours?" inquired Lola.

Carla didn't blink. "Excuse me? Are you trying to make a point?"

Personally, I would have liked to take the badge Carla was still holding and make a point in her head.

Lola said, "Yes, I am. We came in here because we want to know what happened to Ella and Sam's posters. What have you and your zombie army done with them?"

"Posters? Me?" Carla sounded as if cotton candy wouldn't melt in her mouth, never mind butter. "I don't have the slightest idea what you're talking about."

Lola arched one eyebrow. Her voice arched as well. "Don't you? It's probably because you've been so busy having your photograph taken and blowing up balloons. Let me refresh your memory then. The Gerard-Creek posters mysteriously vanished over the weekend."

Carla held her smile like a gun. "And you're accusing *me* of taking them?"

"You bet your last badge I'm accusing you," answered Lola. "Who else do you know would do a thing like that?"

Carla knew someone.

"Quite frankly, I wouldn't be surprised if you took down your posters yourself." Her voice was clear and loud. "It's the kind of cheap trick you're known for."

Lola stood straight for better projection. "No, it isn't. It's the kind of cheap trick you're known for."

Carla went on as though Lola had kept her mouth shut for once. "And there is another candidate—in case you've forgotten." Carla's smile was the smile of a cat with several feathers sticking out of its mouth. "One who's a lot more desperate for votes than I am."

"Morty?" I think I may have gasped.

"Morty didn't do it," snapped Lola. "Morty's a man of honor."

"And you are what?" drawled Carla. "A woman of your word? Because it does come down to that, doesn't it, Lola? Your word against mine."

The common room had stopped being noisy. The silence solidified around us.

Lola opened her mouth and shut it again.

"And how's your friend Stu Wolff these days, Lola?" asked Carla. Stu Wolff was the lead singer of Sidhartha. Lola and I not only had met him and been invited by him to Sidhartha's farewell party, the three of us were picked up by the police together. But such was the duplicitous genius of Carla Santini that no one believed us, of course. "Been to any more of his parties?"

71

12

Sam Has a Carla Santini Experience
of the Third Kind

Carla's campaign went off with a bang. Her posters were everywhere and multiplying faster than amoebas. I was afraid to stand still for more than a second in case someone stuck one on me. They were in the hallways; they were on the windows and the doors; they were on the trees, vending machines, and water fountains. They were even in the restrooms. You shut the door to your stall and there she was, sweetness and light in Kodachrome, suggesting that you vote for her.

Besides the posters, of course, there were the badges. The tiny blue lights flashed like fireflies in the crowd as you walked to your classes.

There were a few Morty Slinger posters around, but next to Carla's they might as well have been drawn with crayons. You only noticed them because they looked so pathetic. Sam said there was still a Gerard-Creek poster in the boys' room in the gym—which brought the grand total left on campus to one.

It was like an election in Stalin's Russia. A visiting alien would have thought that there was only one person running for president.

It wasn't until lunch, however, that I realized that it wasn't just aliens who might think that.

Morty Slinger ran up to me and Lola outside the cafeteria. He was wearing one of his badges. Morty's badges were pretty unique in the history of political gimcracks. Instead of having his name on them, they said SMILE in neon green on a neon pink background. They cost even less than ours.

"What happened?" demanded Morty. "Why did you and Sam drop out of the race?"

I guess you could say that our campaign, in contrast to Carla's, had gone off with a squelch. Morty had to be at least the tenth person that morning to ask me why I'd decided not to run.

"We didn't drop out." I pulled off a few blue and white stars from the poster behind me that were caught in my sweater.

Lola amplified. "Carla just thought Ella and Sam needed more of a challenge, so she made all traces of them disappear."

"Thank God for that," said Morty with a surge of emotion not usually associated with the scientific mind. "I was really worried when I saw all your posters were gone." He looked down at his feet. "I was afraid it might have something to do with Sam."

Lola gave me a look.

"Sam?" I laughed. "What are you talking about?"

"You know . . . because of the pressure and everything . . ." He kicked a fallen Carla badge against the wall. "Because of his record."

The image of an old-fashioned phonograph record appeared in my mind. I wasn't sure what was on it.

"His record?" Confusion made me almost giggle. "What record?"

Morty shuffled. "I'm not trying to find out what it was Sam did—I really don't care. I mean, from the little I've heard it's pretty bad, but—"

There was a flurry of shawl and rattling jewelry beside me. "What's pretty bad?" cut in Lola. "What in the cosmos are you talking about?"

The many interesting features of the floor of the corridor finally lost their hold on Morty's attention. He looked up at us. He blinked.

"Sam's record," said Morty. And then, seeing that this wasn't making us exactly nod with understanding, he added, "You know, his criminal record. Everybody's talking about it."

Now he had *me* blinking. "They are?"

"And exactly what are they saying?" asked Lola.

Morty gaped. "You mean you don't know about it?"

"Of course we don't know about it." Lola's head went up and her voice rose. Bangles beat against each other in rage. "How could we know about it? It doesn't exist."

Morty licked his lips. "That's not what I heard."

"So we gather," said Lola.

Morty's eyes darted back and forth behind his broken glasses; he was ready to run.

"Well?" Lola persisted. "What have you heard, Morty?" She looked like she wanted to shake him.

Farley Brewbaker told Morty that Sam had been arrested and only just managed to stay out of jail. Farley said it could have been a couple of years ago, or it could have been recently. Or it could have been both. Ben Talbot said he'd heard it was something to do with drugs, but Elizabeth Mistle said a reliable source had told her that it was robbery; she thought armed. Somebody else said there had definitely been more than one incident, and a boy in Morty's computer class said he heard that Sam would definitely have been sent away if his mother hadn't been so ill.

"Boy," I said when Morty was through, "that's some story."

"It makes you wonder why we bother reading Aeschylus when there's so much imaginative drama being created right here in Deadwood, doesn't it?" asked Lola.

Morty said, "You mean it's not true?"

Lola groaned. "Of course it's not true. Sam has never committed a criminal act in his life."

She obviously didn't consider stealing Eliza Doolittle's dress a criminal act.

"Well . . . ," Morty rocked from one foot to the other. "You haven't known him all that long . . . Maybe he forgot to tell you."

"He didn't forget to tell us anything," I said. "Those are just rumors, Morty." And malicious ones at that. "They aren't true."

Morty hummed.

Lola put an arm around my shoulder. "Ella and I are Sam's best friends. I think we'd know if he had a murky past, don't you?"

It seemed possible to me that Morty was going to swallow his tongue. Either that or fall over.

"Well . . . ," Morty mumbled. "I mean, you're not necessarily the most reliable witness yourself, are you?"

He was looking over my head, but we both knew which of us he was talking to: Lola. Lying Lola.

"Oh, my God!" Lola pulled away from me. She looked as though she'd actually just caught a glimpse of God, possibly peering out from behind a poster. "Carla Santini! Don't you see? This is all Carla Santini's doing!"

Morty slapped his forehead. "Of course!" He looked really relieved. "How could I be so dense? Carla's already started slinging the mud."

"And now she's going to stop." Lola grabbed my elbow and tugged me toward the door of the cafeteria. "Come on, El."

"But I thought we were going to the computer room to work on our posters."

"We can do that later. First I want a word with your unworthy opponent."

"I'm coming, too," said Morty. "I wouldn't miss this for Stephen Hawking."

76

Naturally, we had no trouble locating Carla Santini in the crowded lunchroom: she was the one under the cloud of balloons.

Carla was sitting with Alma, Tina, and Marcia as usual. They were in the middle of a pretty animated conversation, but Carla, with her witch's instincts, looked up as we neared their table. She didn't so much as blink, even though Lola looked like Lady Macbeth in a really bad mood.

"Well, speak of the devil!" cried Carla, her eyes on me. "I was just saying how much I admire you, Ella— you know, with all these rumors about Sam going around . . ." If she smiled any harder, her teeth would fall out. "A lot of people with less character would have dumped him from their ticket by now."

"How fortuitous that you should mention the rumors," said Lola. "That's exactly what we wanted to talk to you about."

Shock froze the lovely face of Carla Santini for at least half a nanosecond. And then she shrieked a laugh. "Oh, don't tell me . . . you're not blaming me for them, too?" She looked to her fan club, horror in her big blue eyes. "Can you believe it? First they blame me for taking down their posters, and now they're blaming me because Sam Creek's a criminal."

The Santini contingent spluttered with indignation. They'd never heard of such a stupendous outrage. It was a miracle their hair didn't go straight from the shock.

"You deceitful, duplicitous . . ." Lola hesitated, obviously searching for the right word.

"Viper?" suggested Morty.

"Viper!" boomed Lola.

"Name-calling?" Carla tutted. "I thought even *you* were a little more mature than that."

But Lola didn't slow down. "You know perfectly well that you started those stupid rumors." She was speaking very clearly for someone whose teeth were clenched. "Talk about name-calling. The difference between me and you is that you do it behind people's backs."

"No, it's not," said Carla—sweetly but loudly enough to be heard in the hot lunch line. "The difference between me and you is that *I'm* not a liar."

"You're lying now!" howled Lola. I thought she was going for liftoff. "You started those rumors just to discredit Sam."

Carla kept smiling in a serene, almost regal, way. "Says you," said Carla.

"Oh, God . . . ," moaned Alma. "Like anyone would believe Lola, right?"

Someone sitting behind them laughed and said, "Lying Lola."

Carla shrugged helplessly. "You see? Nobody believes a word you say, Lola. Not a single word. They all know better."

And then, from behind us, a sour male voice said, "But they'd believe me."

Lola and I both turned around. It wasn't Morty. It was Sam, smiling his legendary I-don't-give-a-dead-spark-plug smile at Carla Santini.

"Why don't you just tell everybody what they want to know, and we can end this little drama now?" Sam asked her. "Then we won't have all these conflicting rumors. We'll just have the simple truth."

Carla opened her mouth and shut it again. It was a historic moment in Dellwood High history. Carla Santini didn't have an answer.

Sam squeezed in between me and Lola, resting his hands on Carla's table. "What's the matter?" he goaded. "You forget what it was I did? You can't remember what the Dellwood, New Jersey, crime of the century is?"

Carla gave a soft and girlish laugh. "They're just rumors, Sam. They—"

"No, they're not," snapped Sam. "They're totally true." He leaned his face a little closer. "Let me help you out, Carla. Refresh your memory." He really has an amazing smile. "I got into trouble for what I did to a cheerleader in my old school. Her hair grew back, eventually." By now his face was right in hers. "You better watch out, Princess. The mood you've put me in, it could just happen again."

"Bingo!" Lola whispered in my ear. Sam had joined the fray.

13

Desperate Times Call for Desperate Measures

Mrs. Baggoli made Carla leave her balloons out in the hall during English on the grounds that we were reading *Oedipus*, not *Dumbo,* but aside from that brief period in the day, the cloud of silver and blue balloons followed Carla wherever she went. They bobbed above her as she walked through the corridors; they floated over her as she sat in classes; they made it easy for students to find her in the cafeteria—or anywhere else. Which at least meant that we always knew where she was—so she couldn't sneak up and stab us in the back.

"Makes you wish you had a slingshot, doesn't it?" said Sam. He was staring through the door of our headquarters at the room across the hall where the Santini forces were stuffing their faces with free cookies and soda. There were enough balloons outside it to lift a heavy clown.

"David and Goliath," said Lola.

"Except we don't have a slingshot," muttered Sam.

"But that's where you're wrong! We do have a slingshot." Lola pulled a sheet of paper from her bag and held it high. "Behold! Here is our primary weapon of destruction and doom."

"It doesn't look like a slingshot to me," grumbled Sam. "It looks like a poster."

It was a poster. It was straightforward and unassuming, like Sam and me. The background was purple and the lettering was black: GERARD AND CREEK—MAKE YOUR VOTE COUNT.

"What's wrong with it?" I thought it was pretty good, myself. Better than our first six ideas.

"It's meaningless," said Sam. "If the poster's our slingshot, that slogan's a pebble. What we need is a boulder."

Carla Santini's laughter rippled down the hallway like marbles.

"What happened to our issues?" asked Sam. "What happened to 'It's Time to Give Instead of Receive'?"

Lola tore her eyes from the door. "That's all right for speeches and stuff," she explained. "But we need something catchier for the posters."

This wasn't the total reason. The total reason was that Mrs. Turo, who ran the computer room, said it sounded more like a threat than a campaign promise.

Sam stabbed at the poster. "Well, that's not it." Sam has zero tolerance for playing games—which probably isn't a really useful quality in politics—but this time it had worked to our advantage. He was so angry at Carla for starting the rumors about him that every trace of negativity was gone. He wouldn't stop now until Carla was stopped. "It's too vague. Carla's doing everything she can to make this campaign as personal as possible, and I think we should do the same."

I wasn't sure I liked the sound of that.

"Well," I said, "I don't think that the fact that Carla's making it a personal fight means it's okay for us to."

I wasn't even sure if either of them had heard me. Lola already had that look in her eyes.

"You mean roll up our sleeves and get down in the mud?" cried Lola, responding to Sam and not to me. "Pull out her hair? Gouge out her eyes?"

"Smack down!" cried Sam gleefully. "Straight to the mat."

Lola started pacing. "You're right, of course, Sam. We have to fight fire with fire. We have to make an attack."

I didn't like the idea of attack, either. In my opinion, you don't fight fire with fire; you fight it with water. I raised my voice. "I don't see what's wrong with 'Make Your Vote Count.' I think it's catchy. And true. And I'm not really comfortable with attacking Carla personally. I mean, two wrongs don't make a right, do they?"

Lola's voice was louder. "We have to hit her where it hurts. We have to crack through that enormous ego and make the worm within squirm and beg for mercy."

A blue balloon drifted down the hallway. "Kill it before it multiplies!" shouted someone in Morty's room next door. There was a gratifying pop.

"But what about rules, and principles, and stuff like that?" I asked.

Sam put a hand on the back of my chair and leaned

82

toward me. "What is it with you, Ella?" He sounded genuinely curious. "What does Carla have to do to get you mad enough to fight her? She uses your mother, she threatens your life, she takes down our posters—*and* she besmirches my good name—and you don't want to hit her back. Are you a saint, or are you just stupid?"

"Ella's shy and retiring," answered Lola. "She doesn't like too much confrontation. It's not the way she was raised."

Sam shook his head. He looked more baffled than curious now. "How the hell did you wind up with Lola as your best friend if you're so shy and retiring and don't like confrontation?"

I assumed he was making a joke. I laughed. "Don't think it's a question I haven't asked myself."

"You're being unreasonable, Ella," said Lola. "We're not going to do anything despicable and underhanded like Carla would. We're just going to show a little spirit." She climbed on a chair and shook her fist in the air. "We're going to make *issues* an issue, that's what we're going to do." She grinned at Sam. "After we pull out her hair."

"Issues, not image," said Sam.

For a minute there, I almost thought Lola was going to kiss him. I think Sam did, too, because he actually blushed.

"Sam, you're a genius!" Lola was jubilant; triumphant. "'Issues, Not Image!' That's our slogan! That's what we'll do!"

I could tell that she was a few yards ahead of me again. "What's what we'll do?"

Lola didn't even look over at me. "This is so incredibly perfect . . . I can't imagine why I didn't think of this before." She jumped down from her chair, crackling with excitement. "We're totally changing our tactics. We're going to contrast our issues with Carla Santini herself."

I said, "Oh, Lola . . . I don't think Sam meant—"

Sam said, "You what?"

Lola was practically glowing. "For instance—" She ran her hand over an imaginary sign. "We say something like: 'What Have You Done for the World Today?'—and under it we have a photo of Carla putting on makeup."

Sam nodded thoughtfully. "It's good," he decided. "It's clever, and it's funny. It could work."

"Of course it'll work," declared Lola. "It's perfect."

But now Sam was shaking his head. "Back up the truck just a second," said Sam. "How are we going to get a photo of Carla putting on her war paint?"

But there is no problem too great or too small for Lola Cep.

"You've got a camera, haven't you?" Lola asked.

Sam gave her a wary look. "Yeah . . ."

"And you do your own developing, right? So you could print them out the same night."

"Yeah, but . . ."

"And your dad's got a photocopier at the garage, right? So you could run off the posters there."

Sam held up his hand. "Take your foot off the gas, Lola. If you think I'm hiding in the girls' restroom to catch Carla gluing her eyelashes together, you'd better think again."

"Oh, no, not you," said Lola. "You can get the outdoor shots, since you have a car. Ella will get her putting on her makeup."

"What do you mean Ella will do it?" Lola really is too much sometimes. "I'm the presidential candidate, remember? Presidential candidates do not do things like that."

"Oh, really?" said Lola. "What about Watergate? What about Irangate? What about—"

"What about just saying yes, Ella, so we get out of here today," said Sam.

14

Jane Bond and the Incident
at the Dripping Sink

Sam spent Tuesday afternoon following Carla and the coven around Dellwood while Lola and I finished putting up some temporary Gerard-Creek posters.

Instead of using his ancient Karmann Ghia, which was something of a local legend and easily spotted a mile away, Sam borrowed Mr. Colombo's van from his dad's garage, where it was in for service (presumably without asking either Mr. Colombo or Mr. Creek first). The van was most of Sam's disguise—the rest was to wear a jacket borrowed from Lola's mother (had she but known) and a knitted hat to hide his hair. The van was white with the legend COLOMBO'S FINE MEATS on the sides in blue and a painting of a smiling pig underneath it. Sam figured that the driver's seat of a butcher's van was the last place anyone would expect to find a fanatical vegan.

Sam said that although following Carla was a lot less interesting than watching an engine leak, it couldn't have been easier. With no trouble at all, he got several photographs of Carla shopping; several more of her walking down the street, talking on her cell phone; and one of Carla talking on her cell phone while she watched the attendant at the gas station fill her tank.

We needed only one more photograph to complete our set: Carla Santini putting on her makeup.

"I don't understand why you can't do this," I complained as Lola and I left Sam to plaster the first of the new posters all over campus on Wednesday morning. Going along with Lola's crazy ideas was one thing; actually carrying one out on my own was something else. Something nerve-racking and unpleasant. "You're much better at this kind of thing than I am."

Lola swung her book bag over her shoulder with a sigh. "How many times do I have to tell you? Carla expects me to be active and combative, but she doesn't expect that of you. Even if she sees you lurking in the girls' room, she isn't going to get suspicious."

"She will if she sees me hanging over the door trying to take her picture."

"Well, don't let her see you," said Lola. "Be clever. Be subtle. Be spontaneous."

I'm not any of those things. I'm smart enough at schoolwork, but that's not the same as being clever like James Bond. I'm quiet and passive, but that's not the same as subtle, either—it's sort of the same as not being there at all. And you can totally forget spontaneous. My mother is a woman who worries about everything from crumbs to a nuclear holocaust; caution is in my blood.

Lola flapped her shawl, and clanked her bracelets, and steamed on toward the west wing. "Of course you are." She looked over at me, trotting beside her in my lemon A-line. "Anyone with such a fixation on pastels has got to have hidden depths of subtlety."

The entrance to the west wing loomed. Every morning, as soon as she parks her BMW, Carla goes to the girls' restroom in the west wing to touch up her makeup and fix her hair. It's a Dellwood High tradition.

"Shhh!" Lola held up one hand in warning and gently opened the west wing door with the other. "Let me check that the coast is clear."

If you asked me, the coast could only have been clearer if we were in Alaska. It wasn't even eight o'clock yet. The only person on campus besides Sam and us was the janitor.

Lola poked her head through the doorway. She looked left. She looked right. Then she reached back and pulled me after her.

When we got to the girls' room, she did the same thing. Door open, head in, look left, look right, yank Ella in against her will.

"Take the end stall," ordered Lola. "That way she won't see you in the mirror."

I took the end stall.

"You'll have to stand on the toilet," instructed Lola. "So your feet don't show."

I used some toilet paper to lift the seat and stood on the toilet while Lola taped a sign to the door that said OUT OF ORDER. Talk about Watergate. All I could think about was the fact that if my mother were to see me, she'd drop dead on the spot.

Lola stepped back to admire her handiwork. "Perfect." She looked at me. "You've got the camera ready?"

I nodded. Sam's Pentax was in my pocket. Sam set the aperture opening using the light in one of the boys' rooms as a guide so I wouldn't need a flash.

"And you know what to do?"

"I guess so." I eyed the door with a certain amount of misgiving.

"It's easy," said Lola. "You brace one leg in the corner, you hang on to the coat hook with your free hand, and you just pop up and take the picture. Got it?"

I nodded.

She took my book bag and slung it over her shoulder. "That's it, then. I'll see you in homeroom. Don't forget to lock the door."

I'd forget my own name sooner.

It felt as if I were in that stall for days before anyone came into the restroom. They were long, unpleasant days. There was nothing to do but listen to the leaky tap on one of the sinks and—once my feet had gone numb—try not to fall off the toilet.

And worry. There was plenty to worry about. I'm not my mother's daughter for nothing.

What if . . . ? What if . . . ? What if . . . ?

Lola, of course, is never ever bothered by the what-if question. It never occurs to her that something could go wrong with her plans—which is pretty amazing in itself, since something almost always does go wrong with them. But as I crouched on the ceramic rim, the camera in my hand and a cramp beginning in my leg, *What if . . . ? What if . . . ? What if . . . ?* marched through my mind like an invading army.

What if I dropped the camera? What if I fell off the toilet? What if someone told the janitor about the broken toilet and she came to fix it? What if I coughed just as I was about to press the button? What if my mother found out?

But what worried me most was Carla. The sense of empowerment I'd felt when I hung the phone up on her had faded by then. I was back to being normal Ella Gerard, the one who didn't like to make any waves or rock any boats. I knew that taking a picture of Carla putting on lipstick wasn't exactly a major invasion of privacy or anything like that. (There couldn't be many people in Dellwood who had never seen Carla Santini putting her face in place—in the parking lot, on the train, in the supermarket, on the beach, even that time we visited her grandmother in the hospital.) But I knew that Carla would act like it was the biggest invasion of privacy since the white man arrived in the Americas, and the simple truth is that I didn't like people being mad at me—even people I don't like. Carla being mad at me wouldn't depress me the way my parents being mad at me did, but it would make me feel guilty. I was really good at guilt.

What if . . . ? What if . . . ? What if . . . ?

I was just asking myself the question *What if there's a fire and the whole school's been evacuated except me?* when the door to the restroom finally opened and a group of girls burst in, all of them talking at once. I didn't recognize their voices.

And then, a few minutes later, the door opened again.

This time I had no trouble recognizing the voices. Or voice. I could tell that at least three more people had come in, but only one was talking.

"I don't believe it!" The room rippled with rage. Carla Santini was mad. "I don't effing believe it." I could practically hear her curls shaking and see the way her lower lip trembles when she's ready to roll a few heads. "Of all the nerve! Of all the gall! If they think they can treat me like this, they'd better think again."

Sam had obviously put the new posters up all right.

"I just can't believe it!" Carla continued to fume. "I really can't believe it. They're persecuting me, that's what they're doing. They're like stalkers. It's some kind of sick and twisted vendetta." I heard her makeup bag hit the sink. "It's jealousy, that's what it is. Pure jealousy."

I checked that the camera was cocked and made a silent prayer. *Please, let this work . . .* My hands were shaking. It didn't seem possible that no one else could hear the racket my heart was making. All I could think of was how bad I was going to feel if Carla caught me.

Alma Vitters finally managed to squeeze a few words in. "We should talk to Dr. Alsop," she said indignantly.

"This kind of thing has to be against the rules. I mean, we do live in a democracy after all."

"They can't get away with this," agreed Tina Cherry. "They have to be made to pay."

Marcia Conroy said, "If Dr. Alsop wasn't such a pushover, they'd be thrown out of the election for a stunt like this."

"I mean, just what are they trying to insinuate?" shrieked Carla. "That all I care about is shopping? Like none of them ever shops, right? Like the Pope doesn't shop. And what's wrong with shopping, anyway? How can you have a strong economy and a successful nation if people don't shop? If you ask me, shopping is a sign of a truly democratic system. Nobody goes shopping in Cuba, do they? And why not? Because there isn't anything to shop for!"

All the while this acute political analysis was going on, I was trying to get myself in a position where I could rise just enough above the door and go "snap" the way Lola had instructed. Only it wasn't as easy as it sounded.

When my mother took yoga classes, she could balance her whole weight on her hands for minutes at a time, but I was having a lot of trouble balancing my weight on my feet. Of course, my mother hadn't been balancing on the rim of a toilet bowl with a camera. I grabbed for the coat hook, and that's when things totally stopped going according to plan. The coat hook moved. I banged into the door.

One of the advantages of Carla Santini is that when she's going full tilt in the center of the stage, the marines could be landing in the wings and no one would notice. No one heard me hit the door.

"I know whose idea this was," Carla was saying. "It was Lola's."

I've always thought Lola was a pretty name, but on Carla's lips it sounded like something that didn't have legs and oozed slime.

"Sam Creek's a Neanderthal. God knows he could never think of anything like this," continued Carla.

A voice that didn't belong to either Alma, Tina, or Marcia said, "I don't think Sam's a Neanderthal. I think he's kind of cute."

There were a couple of sympathetic giggles, but not from Carla. Carla had dealt with Sam and dismissed him; she had already moved on.

"And as for Ella! Ella practically has to ask permission to breathe. There's no way she could engineer something like this."

I'd been breathing all right without permission up until then, but I nearly stopped completely when I heard my name.

"And Lola has her wrapped around her little finger," chipped in Alma.

"Like a puppet on a string," seconded Tina.

"I wouldn't be surprised if it was more than that," said Carla. She said it as if she knew something; something interesting.

I'd gone back to squatting on the rim, my mission forgotten, but I sat up a little taller at that. I didn't want to miss Carla's next sentence.

I wasn't the only one who was curious.

"What do you mean?" asked Tina, Marcia, and Alma.

Carla hesitated. "Well . . . I'm not saying I know anything for sure . . . It's just—you know . . ."

When Carla Santini says she doesn't know anything for sure, it really means that she doesn't know anything at all.

"Oh, come on," begged Tina, Alma, and Marcia, as though Carla ever kept a secret from them.

"Well . . . I have heard some suspicions . . ." Carla paused again, possibly to put on her mascara; possibly to check her supply of venom. "I mean, they do spend an *awful* lot of time together, don't they? They don't really have any other friends . . . And neither of them has ever had a boyfriend . . ."

I gasped out loud. As far as innuendo went, it seemed to me that Lola came a pretty poor second to Carla Santini. No one heard me gasp, though; there were quite a few gasps out by the sinks.

The girl who didn't think Sam was a Neanderthal butted in again. "I thought Lola was going out with Sam," she said. "They spend a lot of time together, too. And I've seen the way he looks at her."

Carla laughed. "Maybe that's what Lola wants everyone to think. Maybe he's just a beard."

"Beard?" said someone else. "Sam doesn't have a beard."

Carla was amused. "Oh, no, I mean *a* beard. You know, like a disguise."

"You know . . . You may have something . . ." It was Marcia. "I mean, to never have a date . . . and . . ."

One of the other girls laughed, too, but her laugh was nervous. "Are you saying what I think you're saying? You think Lola and Ella—"

I sat there like a cube of ice. What was my mother going to say when this rumor reached her ears? Because it would. Someone would tell their mother; and their mother would tell someone else's mother; and someone else's mother would tell my mother. My parents are liberal, but only to a very limited degree.

"It all makes sense, doesn't it?" said Alma. "I mean, I wouldn't be surprised if Sam Creek was that way, too. He's never dated anyone, either."

"That's because he never speaks to anyone," said the girl who thought Sam was cute.

"That's my point exactly," said Carla. "He's a social deviant."

"What's a social deviant?" asked the girl.

It wasn't Carla who answered. It was someone who hadn't spoken before.

"A social deviant is someone who doesn't obey the laws of Carla Santini, that's what a social deviant is," said Lola Cep.

I was so surprised that I forgot about my mother and Carla being mad at me—all that stuff—and stood up with a lot more sureness now that I was motivated by curiosity and not paralyzed by terror.

Lola was leaning nonchalantly against the door (just out of camera range), and Carla was in the center of the group at the sink. Carla had a tube of lipstick raised in her hand, but her lips were clamped shut.

"And as for suspicious liaisons . . ." Lola must have been listening for quite a while. "If there's anyone who's a couple around here, it isn't me and Ella. I mean, think about it, Carla. You with your stunningly empirical mind can surely see the logic in this. Not only are you and Alma thicker than coagulated blood, but neither of you ever dates the same person more than twice." She laughed girlishly in a perfect imitation of Carla Santini at her most charming. "I mean, what do you think Freud would say about that? Talk about beards! You two could be the Smith Brothers."

There was a spray of giggles, though none of them from Carla or her friends.

"Oh, how droll . . . ," cooed Carla, and she turned back to the mirror to finish her makeup.

It was the perfect moment. Smooth and graceful as a trained killer, I rose over the door and pressed the button.

I couldn't believe I'd done it! I wanted to whoop with joy. I'd done it and no one had noticed a thing. I crouched back down to wait for everyone to leave. I wanted to hug myself, but I was afraid I'd fall off. So I gave the camera a kiss.

Which was when I realized I'd left the lens cap on.

"Let's look on the bright side," Lola said later. "At least you didn't fall in the toilet."

15

More Gauntlets

The call from Dr. Alsop came right at the start of English. I'd never been called to the principal's office before, and I didn't want to go. Lola, of course, wanted to go, but Mrs. Baggoli wouldn't let her.

"I was told to send Ella, not Ella and Lola," said Mrs. Baggoli. She gave Lola a half-smile. "And, unlike some of us, I usually try to do as I'm told."

"It's no big deal," whispered Lola. "It'll be about the posters. You'll be fine."

I must have looked like Oedipus when he realized he'd made a major marital mistake because Mrs. Baggoli gave me a whole smile. "I think it has something to do with the election," she reassured me.

Everybody watched me gather my stuff together and leave the room.

I knew I wasn't really in trouble, but I couldn't help feeling like I was. Sam was waiting for me by the main desk. He was smiling. Sam has spent more time in Dr. Alsop's office than anyone except Dr. Alsop, so this was nothing new for him.

"Cheer up," Sam teased. "They're not going to hang you."

What an optimist.

"Sam! Ella!" Dr. Alsop got to his feet as Ms. Little-moon opened the door. "Come on in." He gestured to the two empty chairs facing his desk. "Take a seat. Take a seat."

There were six visitor's chairs in Dr. Alsop's office. Four of them were already occupied by Carla Santini, Alma Vitters, Morty Slinger, and Farley Brewbaker. Mercifully, Carla had left the balloons outside.

"I'm sorry to have to take you out of class," Dr. Alsop apologized, "but Carla and Alma have a complaint about how the election's being run, and I thought that all the candidates should hear it, too."

Sam and I sat down. I perched uncomfortably on the edge of my chair with my hands on my lap. Sam stretched his legs out and dropped his books on the floor with a thud.

Morty and Farley gave us a can-you-believe-this look, but Carla and Alma ignored us and kept their eyes firmly fixed on Dr. Alsop. Carla wasn't going to let Dr. Alsop know how angry she was; she was playing the innocent victim for all she was worth—which is quite a lot. Alma had her vague, suits-all-occasions smile on her face, but Carla's expression was earnest and concerned. I didn't know if it was true of politicians, but with Carla this was a sign that she was about to start throwing the cow manure around.

Dr. Alsop plopped back in his chair and folded his hands on his desk. "Carla..." He gave her a fatherly smile. "Would you like to tell us what's bothering you?"

It took her a few seconds to get going. She sighed. She shrugged. She twisted a strand of hair around one finger. She crossed her legs. She looked at Dr. Alsop, and then at Alma, and then to heaven (or at least to the ceiling). She said, "Um..." and "Well..." and sighed some more.

"Christ," whispered Sam. "It's like warming up an old car in winter."

Dr. Alsop has been a teacher for decades. He could see the anguish in Carla's face. He knew this was an awkward situation for her, and a difficult one.

"Carla?" Dr. Alsop prompted. His tone was encouraging.

"Well..." Carla sighed. "You know how I hate to make a big production out of things—" Dr. Alsop, bless him, nodded. "Well... it's just that Alma and I are upset by Ella and Sam's new posters. Very upset." She looked over at Alma. "Isn't that true?"

Alma said it was true.

Carla continued to look as if her nails were being pulled out. "If it were just us, Dr. Alsop, we would have let it go—I mean, who has time to get involved in all this petty back-biting?—but several people have asked me about it already, and they're all very shocked, too."

100

Dr. Alsop had been nodding along, looking thoughtful, as a man with all his experience would. Now he said, "And why is that?"

There was a flicker of annoyance in Carla's eyes, but it didn't touch her voice or the gallows smile she turned on Dr. Alsop. "Excuse me?"

"I'm afraid I haven't seen the posters in question," said Dr. Alsop. "Perhaps you could tell me what you find so offensive about them."

Carla explained. She was humble and she was baffled; she couldn't understand why anyone would do a thing like this to her. Our posters made her appear self-centered and shallow. They made her seem unconcerned about the problems of the world.

"As you know, Dr. Alsop, nothing could be further from the truth," concluded Carla. "I mean, my community service record speaks for itself. And if you remember, last year I was given a special award from the Chamber of Commerce."

Dr. Alsop remembered. "I don't suppose you have a sample of these posters with you?"

Do trees have leaves?

"Yes, Dr. Alsop, I do." Carla reached into her book bag and pulled out Exhibit A. "Here."

It was a photograph of Carla and Alma on the main street of Dellwood, their arms filled with shopping and their phones pressed against their ears. Under it was the caption WHERE WILL THEY LEAD US? Beneath that, in smaller letters it said: VOTE GERARD AND CREEK FOR A NEW DIRECTION.

Dr. Alsop gazed at the poster with a bewildered smile. And then he gazed at Carla with a bewildered smile. "I don't understand. Where is Ella and Sam's poster?"

Carla's eyebrows arched shrilly. "That's it, Dr. Alsop. See at the bottom, where it says 'Vote Gerard and Creek'?"

"Good God!" Dr. Alsop laughed sheepishly. "I've seen these. I thought these were your posters, Carla." He laughed again. "Well, what do you know about that?"

"But don't you think it's absolutely outrageous?" Carla demanded. "Do you see what I mean?"

Morty and Farley rolled their eyes.

Dr. Alsop looked at me. "Ella? What do you have to say about this?"

"Well . . ." I licked my lips and took another gulp of air. I felt like I was on trial. *Don't start apologizing,* I told myself. *Whatever you do, don't do that . . .* "Well, I'm really sorry if—"

"Oh, come on, Carla," cut in Sam. "You're going way over the top on this, and you know it. It's no big deal." He turned to Dr. Alsop. "Carla's just pissed off because it's cleverer than anything she's come up with." He grinned in the direction of Carla and Alma. "And more practical than balloons."

Dr. Alsop looked like he was about to smile, but Carla turned to him, too, and he raised a fist to his mouth and coughed instead. His voice was gentle and placating, like a psychiatrist trying to talk a patient down from a ledge. "I understand, Carla—given your outstanding record—that you're upset by what you perceive as—"

"It's not what I perceive," Carla corrected him. Carla Santini would have interrupted Christ during the Sermon on the Mount. "It's what it *says.*"

Morty and Farley rolled their eyes again.

Carla half turned her head, in case there was any confusion about who she was talking to now. "I can't believe you would do something like this to me, Ella." Her voice trembled. "We've been friends for so long."

Even though I knew it was an act, I felt guilt ooze through me.

Everyone was looking at me. I forced myself to speak. "I'm sorry, Carla, I—"

"Do something like what?" It was Sam again. Guilt isn't in his genetic makeup. "That poster doesn't *say* anything. It's up to the reader to decide what it means." He smiled broadly at Dr. Alsop, who seemed to be sucking on his teeth. "Like beauty, it's in the eye of the beholder, isn't it, Dr. Alsop?"

"In the eye of the beholder my aunt Fanny's curlers," said Carla. She was close to letting Dr. Alsop see her claws. "It's a slanderous attack. It's defamatory. It's—"

Dr. Alsop rapped on his desk with his knuckles. Gently. "Carla, I'm afraid I have to agree with Sam on this. I don't really think the poster can be considered slanderous." He cleared his throat and smiled his chummy smile. "It seems perfectly within the bounds of a normal political campaign to me."

"And is that what you think, El?" Carla was looking straight at me now. She was facing away from Dr. Alsop so he couldn't see the lack of girlish warmth in her eyes.

I opened my mouth and shut it again.

Carla smiled. There was no girlish warmth in her smile, either. Not until she returned her attention to Dr. Alsop. "Well," Carla murmured. "I guess maybe I have overreacted."

I heard Morty or Farley say, "Uh-oh . . ."

Dr. Alsop leaned back in his chair. He looked like he was going to say something like "That's the spirit, Carla," but Carla hadn't finished speaking yet.

"But I would like the chance to answer the question the posters raise." She tilted her head to one side. "I do think I'm owed that much."

Dr. Alsop, having thought it was all over, was a little confused. "Well, Carla—" He tapped his fingers against his desk. "Did you have something in mind?"

What a question. It was like asking if birds have wings.

"Well . . ." Carla tilted her head the other way, considering. "I suppose we could have a debate . . . You know, in front of the whole school. Then we could discuss the issues clearly and openly. And I could, you know, correct any wrong impressions."

So that was why we were there. Carla not only wanted to make sure that I couldn't refuse to debate her; she wanted to make sure that the debate itself wasn't the usual after-school affair where the only people who turned up were the candidates and their closest friends. If she was going to wipe the auditorium with me, she wanted to make sure that the auditorium was packed.

Dr. Alsop popped out of his chair like a man on springs. He slammed his palms down on his desk. "That's an excellent idea! Absolutely excellent." He beamed. "I assume no one has any objections?"

"It's all right with us," said Morty.

"Can't wait," said Sam.

Dr. Alsop had obviously given up waiting for me to speak. He clapped his hands together. "Then it's settled. Shall we say a day or two before the election? Give you all time to prepare?"

I smiled, the way a body may smile when rigor mortis sets in.

Two days after the apocalypse would have suited me better.

Alma left right after the meeting, but Carla stayed behind, apparently to give Dr. Alsop some advice about organizing the debate. Morty and Farley, however, needed no prompting to make their exit; they practically ran out of the office. Sam and I were right behind them, Sam checking his watch to see if he needed to bother going back to class.

105

Lola was in the main office, passionately discussing genetically modified food with Ms. Littlemoon, when we came out.

"How'd you get out of English?" asked Sam. "The class isn't over yet."

"Cramps," answered Lola. "They were excruciating. What happened?"

Sam and I told her. In my version, Carla had engineered the whole thing just to get me to debate her because she knew it was my weakest point. In Sam's version, I had risen to the challenge and clanked my blade against Carla's with a merry smirk.

I don't think Lola believed Sam, but it didn't matter. She could only have been more delighted about the debate if she'd gotten me to agree to the idea herself.

"You'll cremate her," crowed Lola. "Maybe we could borrow your dad's camcorder for this. It begs to be kept for posterity."

I begged to be kept for posterity.

"You'll be brilliant. You'll be the Abe Lincoln of Dellwood. We'll give Dr. Alsop a list of the questions we want covered, and I'll coach you till you could answer them in your sleep."

Radar system in perfect functioning order, at that minute Carla stepped through the principal's door, Dr. Alsop hovering behind her with a weary smile on his face.

"Lola!" called Dr. Alsop. "Did you hear the exciting news?"

"It's going to be as major as the Kennedy-Nixon debates," Lola gleefully assured him.

From the expression on his face, I'd guess that he'd already figured this out.

Dr. Alsop went back into his office, probably to collapse, and Carla rolled toward the exit. She stopped when she got to us and tossed her head in a regretful kind of way.

"You know, Lola, it really is a shame you're not running yourself," she purred. She darted a pitying glance in my direction. "You know how much I like a little challenge."

16

Doing What You Must

Except for Morty Slinger, whose campaign tactics couldn't have been more laid-back without the danger of putting him to sleep, after the Showdown at Dripping Sink and the Flinging Down of the Gauntlet, we all threw ourselves into the battle with the zeal of kamikaze pilots.

There was nothing Carla did that we could top. Carla served homemade cookies and designer soft drinks at her after-school gatherings; we countered with organic juice and potato chips. Carla brought her portable CD player in and provided music for her admirers; we brought in Sam's old boom box and played better music but with inferior sound quality. (Morty kept his door shut. He'd turned his headquarters into a computer workshop, filled with science geeks and game heads who didn't like to be disturbed.)

And, predictably, there was nothing we did that Carla didn't top.

Carla's new batch of posters picked up where ours left off. Each featured a picture of Carla doing something wonderful—accepting an award from the Chamber of Commerce, pushing an old lady in a wheelchair, picking up beer cans along a highway—and, tucked off to one side, a photograph of either me, Sam, or even Lola doing something far less wonderful (brushing grass off my skirt, picking his nose, and flapping her shawl, respectively).

We had a rally in the gym one afternoon, attended by such a modest number of supporters looking for food that I not only read my speech without any trouble, but received a round of applause as well (not all of it from Lola). The next day at lunch, the cafeteria was over-taken by varsity cheerleaders screaming, "Give me a C! Give me an A! Give me an R! Give me an L! Give me an A! What's that spell? What's that spell?"

I left the house early every morning so I'd get to school in time to greet potential voters as they arrived. I returned late because, though Sam had to work, Lola and I spent most of each afternoon trying to entice people into our room to drum up support. After supper Lola and I had long phone calls preparing me for the debate. All other spare time that wasn't spent eating, sleeping, or doing homework was spent in coming up with ways to make the students of Dellwood High feel that they were a part of a larger world without volunteering them all for the Peace Corps. We would raise money for worthwhile causes; we would adopt a family at Christmas; we would sponsor an exchange student from an underdeveloped country; we would organize volunteers to help junior high students with reading and math.

Despite the fact that every major campus person-ality—members of the football teams, the basketball teams, the cheerleaders, and just about anyone else whose yearbook caption would include "sure to suc-ceed"—was backing Carla, by the end of the first week of campaigning (or Round One, as Sam called it), Lola was convinced—either from her creative intuition or from counting badges, I wasn't sure which—that Carla and I were neck and neck.

Personally, it felt more like my neck was broken. By the weekend, all I wanted to do was lock myself in my room and not speak to anyone until Monday morning.

Fat chance, with Lola around. She turned up first thing Saturday morning, ready to teach me how to win the debate. It was all uphill.

"The two most important things to remember," said Lola, during our third break, "are, one: you don't have to answer the question you've been asked and—"

"So what do I answer? The question I haven't been asked?"

"Exactly. You answer the question you can answer. It's what all politicians do. Someone asks the president about, say, national medical insurance, and because he doesn't want to lose the votes of doctors or of people who want national medical insurance, he talks about all he's done to fight pollution."

It was starting to work; that actually made some weird sort of sense.

"What's the second important thing?"

"That nobody expects you to tell the truth."

"They don't?"

"Of course not. They expect you to tell them what they want to hear."

"They do?"

"Absolutely. Look at George W. Bush. Look at Bill Clinton. Look at George Bush Senior. George Bush Senior was the best. He even said, 'Read my lips: No new taxes,' and then the next thing anybody knew, new taxes. But nobody goes around saying, 'God, what a liar!' People still love him."

I share a gene pool with two of the people who still love George Bush Senior.

I rested on my elbows. In Lola's bedroom, we always sit on the floor because her bed is piled with clothes and cookie boxes and stuff like that; in my room, of course, we sit on the floor because of my mother's bed thing, and we don't eat because of my mother's thing about no food outside of designated areas (the kitchen, dining room, or patio).

"But I thought I'm meant to be the anti-Santini—"

"Oh, for God's sake, El . . ." Lola went prone, decimated by the experience of trying to educate me in the finer points of political behavior. "I'm not saying you have to *lie*." She sat up, now leaning toward me with urgency. "This isn't supposed to cause a moral dilemma, you know. It's supposed to make things easier. All I'm saying is that you can lie if you need to. And that you don't have to worry about not being able to answer a question, because you don't have to answer anything you don't want to answer—just answer something else. It's really easy."

Sighing, I lay back on the carpet. "I don't know if I can remember everything. I'm exhausted." My brain hurt from thinking so much, and my voice hurt from talking so much, and all of me hurt from the stress of keeping it all together. And I wasn't sleeping that well, either. Everyone had always been amazed that my parents never argued, but after sixteen years of living with them, I'd finally found out that they did argue—but only in the dead of night. I don't know how many times in the past few days I'd woken up to the sound of shouting. I'd thought it was someone's TV at first.

"Well, you can bet your last maxi pad that Carla will remember."

"Carla doesn't have to remember. Manipulating the truth is second nature to her."

"First nature," corrected Lola. She straightened up suddenly, looking toward the window. "Did you hear a car?"

I didn't hear a car, but now that I was listening, I heard a car door slam shut.

"It must be my dad."

"It's a little early for Mr. Darling, isn't it?" asked Lola. "It's still daylight."

One of Lola's theories about my father's hardly ever being home was that he was a vampire and only emerged from his coffin when it was dark.

And then we heard my mother's voice at the front door. She was gushing like a fountain. "Why, Carla! What a lovely surprise. I'm afraid you caught me up to my elbows in puff pastry." Carla laughed in delight. "I was just saying to Ella the other day," my mother gushed on, "that we don't see enough of you anymore. I told her she should invite you over. We don't see you nearly enough."

I went rigid with attention. I didn't like the sound of that. It was too effusive. And my mother's voice was a little mushy. Could she have moved cocktail hour back?

"Good God!" cried Lola in a hoarse whisper. "It's the Santini!"

I reached the door first. It wasn't that I'd become a snoop; but I had to keep at least an ear on my mother. Just in case.

We tiptoed toward the head of the stairs.

"Actually, it's you I came to see," Carla was saying. "I have a really big favor to ask."

Lola and I exchanged a look.

"Probably the head of her firstborn," whispered Lola.

It was no time for joking. My mother had just invited Carla into the kitchen, where they could talk. And where the wine would be. All we could hear was "Oh, please say yes. You know you're the best cook in Dellwood." Carla's voice sounded as if her hands were clasped. "And it would be so cool."

My mother laughed again. "I'm not sure Ella would think it was so cool . . ."

"Oh, Ella won't mind," Carla assured her. "It's not like we're enemies, Mrs. Gerard. We're just opponents."

"Yeah . . . ," muttered Lola. "Like God and Satan."

"Well . . . ," My mother sighed as if she was weakening. "Are you sure it wouldn't be easier to have a barbecue?"

"Good Lord!" breathed Lola. "The brazen hussy. She's hiring your mother to cook for her."

"Shhh . . . !"

"Barbecues are boring," Carla said. "I want something really special. Something that symbolizes my beliefs."

Lola choked. "What's she want her to make? A neutron bomb?"

This time I stepped on her heel. "Shhh...!"

Carla was now talking about spring rolls, samosas, and tostadas. She'd already roughed out a menu.

"I want as many different countries represented as possible," summarized Carla. "After all, we are a global village now, aren't we, Mrs. Gerard? I mean, we don't just live in Dellwood, New Jersey, anymore. We live in Calcutta, Beijing, and Mexico City as well. Our culture stretches across the globe."

"She means McDonald's stretches across the globe," muttered Lola.

"Shhh . . . !"

"Right," said my mother. "You're absolutely right. The world doesn't begin and end with Dellwood, New Jersey, does it?" She sounded as though this was one of the most important pieces of information she'd ever heard.

"Of course it doesn't. We're one world now," intoned Carla. "That's what my campaign is all about. That's why everybody who comes to my rally has to dress up like someone from a different country, and I want the food to be from everywhere. You know, like a smorgasbord of international cuisine. Including from the States."

Lola and I exchanged another look. What rally?

My mother was still murmuring to herself. "You're right . . . Millions—billions—of people live in places that aren't Dellwood. This isn't all there is."

"Is your mother going through a midlife crisis or something?" whispered Lola.

It was more upmarket wine than midlife crisis if you asked me.

"*Shhh . . . !*"

Carla gamely carried on. "You know, from different regions. Fried chicken from the South . . . that kind of thing . . ."

My mother said, "Fried chicken?"

"Maybe we should just concentrate on the rest of the world," said Carla.

"Well . . ." My mother sighed. "It would certainly be a challenge."

"Say yes," begged Carla. "I love a good challenge. Don't you?"

17

Unexpected Complications

Carla's rally replaced the election itself as the main topic of conversation at school the next week. Carla was calling it a rally, but it had as much to do with an ordinary rally as a grade school hop has to do with a high school prom. In fact, from what we heard, it seemed likely that Carla's one-world rally was going to put the prom in the shade. Not only was it being catered by Marilyn Gerard, but there was to be a live band, fireworks, and a prize for the best costume as well. Sam called it the Million-Dollar Bash.

Because of the excitement over Carla's rally, we had a grand total of three visitors to our headquarters all week, and two of them were looking for Morty. Our third visitor was Morty himself. Carla was throwing the Million-Dollar Bash for her friends and supporters, and Morty was having the Poor Boys' Potluck Picnic on Saturday night in his backyard for everybody else. He came by to invite us along.

Even though it meant the debate was that much closer, I was grateful when Friday came, since at least it would soon be over.

"Maybe we could poison the food," suggested Sam as we passed yet another gaggle of girls asking each other what they were wearing Saturday night. "That should cut some of her votes."

"Now, that's tempting," said Lola. "Strychnine in the samosas . . . cyanide in the corn fritters . . . But then Marilyn would get blamed." She sighed. "She would never recover. Suburban murders always get a lot of press attention."

"Thanks for thinking of my mother's feelings."

"Well, it's not as if she thinks of yours," said Lola.

"Maybe you could convince your mother to bail out of the catering at the last minute," Sam suggested. "Tell her you regard it as an act of betrayal."

Even if I felt that I could have told my mother not to, I wouldn't have. My parents had a big fight the weekend before, but the rally had cheered her up. She couldn't have been more excited if it were a party of her own. As far as I was concerned, she could have it at our house if it made her happy.

"Forget it, Lola. My mother wouldn't let Carla down for anything."

"It's too bad she doesn't feel that strongly about you," said Lola.

*   *   *

Lola and I had a weekend of serious hard work planned. The big debate was the following Thursday, the day before the election. Maybe Carla Santini wanted to fritter the time away, dancing and eating authentic Thai spring rolls, but I was going to work on my arguments and hone my rhetorical techniques, so that on Thursday I could dazzle the school with my debating skills—and wipe the auditorium with Carla Santini. As Sam said, after Carla's party it would be the only chance I had.

I stayed over at Lola's on Friday night as usual, and on Saturday she came home with me.

My mother's car was in the driveway when we got to my house, but my father's car wasn't. All systems normal.

"Mom?" I called as we stepped through the front door. "Mom? I'm home."

"She must be in the kitchen," said Lola. "Pilfering the cuisines of the world for Carla's party."

"Mom, I'm back!" I pushed the swinging door, and Lola and I stepped into the kitchen.

"Good God!" breathed Lola. "What is this? A parallel world?"

I could only hope so.

I had never in my life seen our kitchen (or any other room in our house) in a state that was less than perfect. As Lola often said, God has ten commandments, but my mother has over a hundred—and a good thirty of them concern the kitchen. Do not leave dirty dishes in the sink. Put anything you're not using away. Clean up after yourself.

I looked from the dirty dishes in the sink to the food and used utensils that seemed to have been hurled around the room. The apron my father gave my mother as a joke Christmas present (TOO MANY KISSES SPOIL THE COOK was written across the front) was lying in a corner, looking stepped on.

A few more of my mother's commandments occurred to me. Never ever smash eggs on the cupboard doors. Do not splatter the refrigerator with salsa. Do not attack the microwave with a plate of spicy vegetable fritters. Never leave peanut sauce burning on the stove.

"Maybe she's been abducted by aliens," suggested Lola. She put on a reading-the-tabloids voice. "Suburban mother taken aboard an alien spacecraft while preparing Southeast Asian food."

"I doubt it."

There was an empty wine bottle on the table. Alien abduction seemed unlikely.

Lola took her eyes from the scene of furious destruction to see what I saw on the table. Then she turned her eyes on me. "Is there something you forgot to tell me, Ella?"

I shrugged. "It's no big deal . . . but sometimes she does mistake the chardonnay for water."

Lola frowned as though trying to concentrate. "Are you saying your mother, Marilyn Gerard, is an alcoholic? Is that what you're saying?"

"She isn't an alcoholic," I said firmly. "She just drinks too much. Sometimes." I glanced at the eggs streaming

119

down the cabinets like melting eyes. "When she's unhappy."

And she was definitely unhappy now.

Lola whistled under her breath. "That's why you were so good when Stu Wolff was so drunk, isn't it? Because you're used to dealing with Marilyn."

"I suppose so." That was why we'd been picked up by the police: because Stu Wolff was so drunk. I smiled feebly. "I have had practice."

"My God . . ." Lola was shaking her head in an awed kind of way. "Maybe you're the one who should be the actress, Ella. How long has this been going on?"

I gave another shrug. "I don't know. Awhile. It sort of snuck up on me."

"The way things do," said Lola. Her eyes wandered around the room again. "Do you think you'd better look for her? Make sure she's all right?"

"She's probably asleep."

I went over to turn off the scorched sauce. That's when I noticed the letter. It was lying on the table by the bottle, a torn envelope, soaked with wine, beside it. Lola noticed it, too.

"What's that?" asked Lola. She came and looked over my shoulder. *"Dear Marilyn,'"* she read. "Is that your dad's handwriting?"

I put my hand over the letter. "You can't read other people's mail, Lola. It's against the law."

Lola nudged me out of the way. "Oh, for pete's sake, El. That's in normal circumstances. In normal circumstances, everyone has a right to privacy. But these aren't normal circumstances. Your father isn't exactly a letter man, is he? He's more an e-mail and fax man." She snatched up the piece of paper. "This could explain what happened. You want to read it, or shall I?"

I didn't try to snatch it back. It was unusual for my father to write a letter—as unusual as coming home to find that Hurricane Marilyn had swept through the kitchen—and for once I actually agreed with Lola. Something really awful must have happened. Since I was obviously the one who was going to have to clean up the mess, I figured I had a right to know what that something was.

"We'll read it together."

She gave me a look. "You're sure? I don't want to butt in. I mean, it is your family thing."

I was touched by the lie. Lola is the premier butter-inner of all time. If she'd been around when God was creating the world, she'd have given *Him* advice. But it wasn't sentiment that made up my mind; it was my mother. Among my mother's million rules is the one about not talking about the family to outsiders—which is everyone else. I'd been obeying that rule all my life. Always worrying what people thought, or said, or might do. In fact, my family worked so hard at appearing perfect that we didn't even talk to each other. I hadn't even said a word to my father about my mother's drinking habits—and he'd never said a word to me. Of course, before I met Lola, there wouldn't have been anyone else to tell anyway. My parents' friends weren't the kind you talked to when you were in trouble, and neither were mine. But now I did have Lola, and that made a difference.

"I'm sure."

We read the first line standing up: *Dear Marilyn, I don't think this will come as any surprise . . .*

We glanced at each other. It was a surprise to me and Lola. And from the state of the kitchen, it was probably a surprise to my mother, too.

"We'd better sit down," said Lola. "This is definitely heavy."

We sat down.

My father wasn't going to be home this weekend. Or the next weekend, either. My father had taken "the job in London after all." So they could "have a breather." So they had "space in which to think."

"My God, trouble in paradise . . . ," whispered Lola. "The Darlings need space . . . I didn't think they ever even argued." She looked me straight in the eye. "Did you know any of this?"

It was all news to me. *What job in London? Breather from what?*

I shrugged. "You know my parents; they always act like everything's fine." They were like Carla Santini: image was all.

I'll leave it to you to explain things to Ella, wrote my father. *I'll call in a couple of days.*

"Well, that was nice of him," said Lola. "He could have talked to you himself."

"How could he talk to me?" My voice was a little shrill. "He's never home."

"They have phones in New York as well as London," said Lola.

I picked up the envelope. My father had mailed the letter from his office on Thursday. By the time my mother got it, he was already unpacked and over his jet lag.

Lola and I just sat there for a while, looking from the letter to each other, and back again. I was definitely in shock. And I was starting to change my mind about the Greeks. "'Count no man happy until he is dead . . .'" Truer words were never spoken. And count no teenage girl happy, either.

I'm not a doer, like Lola; I'm a waiter. I could have sat there for hours, waiting to see what would happen next, but there was a crash in the hallway, and someone muttered something that sounded a lot like "Damn it!" What was happening next had already started to happen.

Lola looked at me. "I guess she isn't asleep."

"Quick." I pulled Lola out of her chair. My mother wasn't going to exactly jump for joy if she found out what we'd done. "Act like we haven't seen the letter."

"Should I act like I haven't seen the kitchen, either?"

"Just follow my lead for once, okay?"

By the time my mother stumbled into the kitchen, we had our heads in the refrigerator, looking for a snack.

"Ella, honey!" My mother laughed in surprise. "I didn't know you were home. I'm so glad you're here." Her voice was on the thick, slurred side.

"We just got in," I said quickly. I looked around. There was some sauce on her blouse, but she looked a lot better than the kitchen. At least she seemed to be standing all right.

My mother gave me a bleary smile. "I have to find my passport, honey. Do you know where my passport is?" She had an opened bottle of wine in one hand and an empty glass in the other.

"Hi, Mrs. Gerard," said Lola. "How's the cooking going?" You would never know from her smile or her voice that she knew she was standing on eggshells.

I couldn't tell whether my mother even saw Lola or not, but she definitely didn't hear her.

"I have to go to London," said my mother. She poured herself another drink and thumped the bottle down on the sideboard. "Do you know where my passport is?"

"Mom?" I walked toward her, trying not to step on anything and seem nonchalant at the same time. "What about the party, Mom? Do you need some help?"

My mother had yanked open the drawer of the sideboard and was dumping things on the floor. "I have to find my passport," said my mother. "I have to go to London."

I laughed. Brightly and lightly. "You can't go today, Mom. It's Carla's party tonight, remember?"

My mother told us what her present opinion of Carla's party was.

Lola gasped. "I didn't think Marilyn even knew that word," she whispered.

"Mom." She'd finished emptying out the drawer and was pouring herself more wine. "Why don't you sit down and rest for a few minutes?" I tugged her toward a chair. "I'll look for the passport after I've made some coffee."

She still had the glass and the bottle in her hands, but she obediently sat down, staring at the wall like Zombie Mom.

Lola rolled her eyes. "Just point me toward the coffee," said Lola. "I'll do it."

I sat down beside my mother. "Mom? Are you all right?"

With effort, my mother focused on me. There was another second of blankness, and then she remembered who I was.

"Ella, honey!" She blinked. "Ella, have you seen my passport?"

I put my hand on hers. "I'll find the passport," I promised. "But right now you have to think about Carla's party. It's tonight, remember? Lola and I will help."

My mother repeated that she was looking for her passport. Her voice was close to crying. "I have to go to London," she informed me. "I have to talk to your father."

I kept my own voice soft and gentle, as though I were talking to a small child, or possibly a cat. "You can't go now, Mom. It's Saturday, remember? Carla's party is tonight. She's counting on you."

My mother emptied her glass again. "I have to find my passport. I'm going to London. I have to talk to your father."

I patted her hand. "But he's going to call. Remember? Remember he said he'd call? Why don't you wait till Dad calls?"

I thought she might realize that I didn't officially know that he'd promised to call, but she didn't. She pushed off my hand. "London." She filled her glass again. Considering the rate at which she was drinking, she might as well have drunk from the bottle. "I'm going to London. You'll be all right."

"But Dad wants to talk to you," I coaxed. "And Carla's par—"

"And I want to talk to him." She nodded as though agreeing with herself. "That's what I have to do. I have to talk to your father."

"That's why you should stay here. So you can talk to him when he calls."

Another glass of wine joined the others. She grabbed hold of the table and pushed herself to her feet. None too steadily. "I am going to talk to him," said my mother. "I'm going to London. He can't do this to me."

There was no point in saying that he had done this to her. And there was no point in saying "What about me?" When my mother was like this, the entire population of the planet shrank to one. But patience usually worked. I stood up, too, and tried again.

"But he's calling soon. He really wants to talk to you. Don't you want to be here when he calls?"

"Your father," said my mother. "Did you know your father has gone to London?"

126

"Yes, I know he's in London." I smiled encouragingly. "But he's going to call. He wants to talk to you."

My mother swayed. "I have to find my passport. I have to go to London." She pitched herself toward the door.

It was Lola who caught her before she hit the floor. She wasn't unconscious, but she wasn't exactly conscious, either.

"She's heavier than she looks," grunted Lola.

I got on the other side of my mother and put her arm over my shoulder. "She'll sleep now," I whispered. "If we can get her upstairs. We can take the back way."

At least then the worst would be over.

We started more or less dragging my mother across the kitchen to the back staircase.

The doorbell rang.

"Don't answer it," advised Lola. "They'll go away."

The doorbell rang again. Impatiently. Whoever it was wasn't going away.

"Get the phone, Ella," mumbled my mother.

"Mrs. Gerard?" It was Carla Santini, of course, shouting through the mail slot. Her projection's even better than Lola's. "Mrs. Gerard? It's Carla."

I'd been wrong again.

The worst wasn't almost over. The worst was about to begin.

18

In the Time-Honored Greek Tradition
Things Go from Bad to Much Worse

Carla Santini was standing on the front porch with a box in her hands and a "Vote Carla" badge pinned to her blouse. It was flashing.

She's like the buzzard of bad news, I thought. *She starts circling overhead at the first whiff of trouble.*

"Hi, Ella." Carla treated me to one of her NutraSweet smiles. "I promised your mom I'd stop by." She added saccharine to the NutraSweet. "You know, last-minute conference before my rally." She risked a few wrinkles in middle age by making a face. "No wonder presidents always get so old while they're in office. I mean, I haven't even been elected yet, and there is sooo much to do—planning . . . organizing . . . decisions—"

Lying . . . scheming . . . spending all that money . . .

Carla broke off with a humble laugh. "Listen to me, explaining to you. You must know as much about it as I do."

And then some, I thought. But all I said was "Right." I couldn't think of anything else to say.

"So?" said Carla. "Are you going to ask me in?"

"Of course." I didn't so much as twitch. "Only . . . only I'm afraid my mother doesn't want to be disturbed right now. You know, she's right in the middle of everything."

"This won't take long." Not a person who needs any encouragement, Carla stepped past me and into the hall. Short of tackling her, there wasn't any way to keep her out. Carla held up the box. "I brought over the costumes for your mom and Mrs. Wallace." My mother always hires Mrs. Wallace to help her set up her parties and dinners.

"Oh." I laughed. "I didn't know they were wearing costumes."

"Everybody's wearing a costume," Carla assured me. "Even my parents and their friends. It's going to be like the United Nations."

Any time I'd seen a meeting of the United Nations on television, everyone was dressed in suits, but I didn't comment. I reached out for the box. "I'll make sure she gets it."

Carla pulled it out of my reach. "That's okay, I'll give it to her. I'm dying to see what she's making." She soaked me with another smile. "You and your dad are sooo lucky. Your mother is such a great cook."

"I'm afraid I have to insist," I insisted. "You don't know my mother. She doesn't like to be disturbed when she's working." I slowly edged myself between Carla and the hallway that leads to the kitchen. "It throws off her timing." I leaned against the wall. "Timing is crucial in cooking."

Carla wasn't interested in cooking. Why should she be? She wasn't ever going to have to do any herself. But she was interested in something.

"What's that?" asked Carla. "Don't tell me you got a dog."

I followed her eyes to the bottom of the stairs where a large wet patch had darkened the carpet. So that was why my mother swore when she came downstairs; she spilled her wine.

I made my face blank. "No," I said flatly, "we didn't get a dog."

One eyebrow arched ever so slightly. "Your mother really must be busy if she didn't notice that." She knew my mother well enough to know that the most infinitesimal speck of dust didn't fall in our house without my mother noticing. She gave me another smile. "So what is it?"

I said the first thing that came into my mind. I said, "It's probably from when she watered the plants."

It was the wrong thing to say.

"What plants?" asked Carla. "Your mother hates indoor plants."

It was true—my mother said they attracted bugs. It's Lola's mother who has plants all over the house.

"She's mellowing," I said. "She likes them now."

Carla looked suspicious. I could almost see her ears prick up. "Really?" She sniffed. Maybe she wasn't the buzzard of bad news after all. Maybe she was the bloodhound of doom. "It doesn't smell like water."

"Doesn't it? I don't know what else it could be."

Even Carla Santini wasn't going to get down on the floor for a closer inspection right in front of me. But she didn't have to; I could tell she could tell I was lying.

Carla sighed. "Well, I guess you can't fight city hall, can you?" She waved the box at me. "I'll just give this to her, and then I'll be on my way."

She started to move toward the door at the end of the hall.

"She's not in the kitchen!" I may have screamed. "She's—" Carla turned to look at me. "She's upstairs."

Carla tilted her head. "I thought you said she was busy cooking."

"She is busy cooking," I rushed on. "But she likes to take little breaks. You know, power breaks." If anyone in the world could understand the concept of power breaks, that person had to be Carla Santini.

Carla stared at me for a second. Coldly. And then she shrugged. "Well, that's okay. You can give me a coffee while I wait."

I said, "I . . ."

Carla smiled.

I said, "Well . . ."

Carla smiled some more.

I said, "I think she has a headache."

"A headache?" Carla stopped smiling. "You didn't mention a headache before."

Hanging out with Lola was paying off; the lies were coming thick and fast.

"I didn't want you to feel guilty." As if Carla Santini even knows what guilt is. "You know, because she got it from working so hard for your rally."

"Really? How thoughtful of you." Her eyes darted toward the stain again. She hadn't missed the wine bottle in the kitchen the other day. "Well, what if I just pop up to see her? It won't take more than a couple of minutes."

I was really beginning to understand the Greeks now. Lola was right; I was a product of my environment. I was brought up by people who planned, followed rules, and were insured against everything from fires and floods to things falling out of planes and being hit by an asteroid. They believed that if they took the proper precautions, they could protect themselves from anything bad. And I'd believed that, too. But if I'd been raised by Aeschylus, I would have known better. I'd have known that bad things happen no matter how much insurance you have.

Standing there, watching Carla about to launch herself up the stairs to find no one there, I consoled myself with the thought that at least things were about as bad as they could get.

But if I had been raised by Aeschylus, I would also have known that no matter how bad things are, they can always get worse.

Carla had one foot on the stairs when the bottom fell out of the bad news box.

"Carla, honey?" my mother's voice called down the stairs.

132

There was no thickness or slur in it now.

Carla was as surprised as I was, though she didn't go into cardiac arrest. She gave me a suspicious glance and rallied immediately. "Hi, Mrs. Gerard!" she called back. "I just wanted to see how things are going. And I brought your costumes."

My mother's voice was slightly muffled, as if she had a bag over her head. Or a towel. "I just got out of the shower." She laughed the distinctive Marilyn Gerard laugh; hee-hee-hee. "I needed to reenergize myself. There's still a lot to do. And I'm sure you must have a million things to do yourself . . . Why don't you just leave the costumes with Ella, honey? I'll talk to you later."

Carla was craning her neck up the stairs, where there was nothing to see, her expression thoughtful. "Sure," said Carla. "The rally starts at eight, so I'll see you at six, Mrs. Gerard. That should give you enough time to set everything up."

"Six o'clock," echoed the voice of my mother. "See you then, honey."

I could hear Lola on the phone in the kitchen as I came down the stairs.

"It's an emergency," she was saying. "I don't care whose car you're under, you have to get over here pronto."

She was silent for a few seconds while Sam gave in.

"Great," said Lola. "Oh, and—Sam? Could you pick up some chips and pretzels and stuff like that on the way? A lot. Enough for a hundred . . . Ella will pay you back when you get here."

She was silent for one second while Sam wondered aloud why she wanted a lot of potato chips.

Lola looked up as I came into the kitchen. "I'll tell you when you get here. Ella and I have a lot to do." She hung up the phone. "Well?" she said to me. "How's Marilyn?"

"Out like a light."

"Excellent." She handed me the broom. "You start on the floor. I'll tackle the counters."

I took the broom. Reluctantly. "You do realize that this isn't going to work, don't you?"

"Well, use the mop then," said Lola.

I heaved a sigh worthy of Lola Cep. "No, I didn't mean the broom. I meant Plan A."

Plan A was a typical Lola Cep plan; simple but impossible. Lola and I, wearing the costumes intended for my mother and Mrs. Wallace, would take the food that my mother had already prepared to Carla's party in my mother's car. There was nothing about Plan A that couldn't go wrong. It had more scope for disaster than a nuclear war.

"And what are you putting forth as Plan B?" she inquired. "Telling the truth? Because that's the only other feasible option I see. There is no choice."

"Well, if we have no choice, it's because somebody opened her big mouth."

"I don't believe this!" Lola flapped the garbage bag she'd taken from under the sink in my direction. "That's

134

gratitude for you, isn't it?" she squawked. "If I hadn't stepped in, Carla would have been up the stairs looking for Marilyn in less time than it takes to say 'social outcasts.' Unless, of course, you were planning to tell Carla that working so hard for her rally had made your mother invisible."

I swiped at the floor with the broom. "Well, maybe next time you should try *not* to help." I was snarling slightly. "If you were going to pretend to be my mother, why couldn't you have a major migraine that would incapacitate her for days?"

Lola wasn't snarling; she was the voice of reason. "Because Carla was suspicious. I could hear it in her tone." She started sweeping debris from the counter into the bag. "Correct me if I'm wrong, but I was under the impression you wouldn't want Carla to discover the truth. I know I don't. The last thing we need is to actually give her something to talk about. It's worse than when she has to make things up."

It wasn't easy to argue with that, but I tried. "I still think a migraine would have worked."

"Then why didn't *you* say Marilyn had a migraine?" countered Lola.

"I did say she had a headache."

"You also said she was too busy to be disturbed."

"I'm not used to lying the way you are. I said the first thing that came into my head."

"Well, it's too late for your mother to develop a migraine now." Lola's voice was heavy with scorn—

presumably for me, the mediocre liar in the group. "Carla would be round here with a news team. She'd know for sure then that something is up."

Lola was right about that, too, of course. If my mother didn't arrive with the food, Carla would be on me like a hawk on a mouse.

"And anyway," Lola went on, "my plan will work. You just have to believe."

"I do believe. I believe that I'd rather be dead."

"Oh, don't be so melodramatic," ordered Lola. "It's going to be a piece of cake."

"But you're shorter than my mother."

"I'll wear heels."

"And you're heavier."

"They'll think it's the costume."

"And I'm taller and thinner than Mrs. Wallace."

"Mrs. Wallace is the help. Carla's not going to notice if she's gained a couple of inches or lost a few pounds."

"And she wears glasses."

"So will you," Lola assured me. "Sam's going to stop by my house and get my stage glasses."

"Well, what about the food?" I had a really bad feeling about how this evening was going to turn out. "We don't have enough food."

Lola's sigh made mine sound like the breath of a butterfly. "Well, that's why Sam's bringing the chips, isn't it, Ella? So we'll have plenty to eat."

"Pretzels and potato chips aren't exactly part of an international buffet," I argued.

"Oh, for God's sake, El. Your mother's the only person on the planet who doesn't think snack food is fit for human consumption. The rest of the country lives on it. As long as they've got something to stuff in their faces, they're not going to notice whether it's Indonesian egg rolls or nacho chips."

"But you just can't—"

I was going to say you just can't go around impersonating people, but Lola didn't give me a chance to finish.

"Can't . . . Can't . . . Can't . . . ," she chanted. "That should be your middle name: Ella You-Just-Can't-Do-That Gerard. That's your first reaction to everything."

"Well, in this case it's true!" I wailed. "You just can't pretend to be somebody else."

"Maybe you should become a cloistered nun," said Lola. "Then you really couldn't do anything but obey orders."

I may be a coward, but I'm a stubborn one. "But what about my mother? What if she wakes up while we're gone?"

Lola raised her arms to implore the heavens, dumping all the garbage she'd taken from the counters onto the floor.

"For pete's sake, El. What do you think I called Sam for?"

"To pick up the chips and the glasses?"

"That, too." Lola smiled as though she'd just invented the wheel. "Sam's going to mommy-sit while we're out."

I practically dropped my broom. "And does Sam know this?"

"Not yet," said Lola.

Lola was finishing off the kitchen and I was finishing off lying to Mrs. Wallace when Sam arrived with the stage glasses and a hundred bags of chips and pretzels.

"I said a lot, not everything they had," said Lola.

Sam said, "So what's going on?"

We told him what was going on while we changed into our costumes. I explained about my mother; and Lola explained Plan A. Sam didn't bother to argue. I think he was probably so flabbergasted by the news that my mother was "sleeping it off" upstairs that he would have said yes to cutting his hair.

All he said when we were through was, "You know, Lola, I never knew how dull my life was until I met you."

But Sam's easy acquiescence didn't mean that he thought any more of Plan A than I did. As far as that went, Sam agreed with me.

"You're nuts," he shouted through my bathroom door. "You can't do this, Lola. It isn't going to work."

Lola rolled her eyes in my direction. "Good God," she muttered, "he sounds like *you*."

I, however, was too busy staring at my reflection in the mirror to pay much attention to what Lola was doing. My reflection was pretty gripping.

"I'm not going," I whispered. "I can't be seen in public like this."

138

For my mother, the elite caterer, Carla had chosen an elaborate geisha outfit from the upper end of the costume market. For Mrs. Wallace, the hired help, she'd selected the cheapest thing she could find, which as far as I could tell was meant to be Hawaiian. It featured a plastic grass skirt, half a dozen plastic leis, a pink body suit, and a black wig made from the hair of a horse that had died a terrible death. All that was missing was a bra made out of coconuts.

Lola didn't let my declaration disturb her conversation with Sam for a nanosecond.

"O ye of little faith!" she cried, raising her eyes to the ceiling light. "Why am I given only doubters?"

"This is reality speaking, not doubt!" Sam shouted back. "Unless there's a blackout, you're not going to fool anyone for more than a minute."

Lola stepped away from the sink, scrutinizing herself in the mirror. She looked incredible. Even her own mother wouldn't have recognized her. I half expected Lola to start pouring tea.

"That's what you think." She smiled. "Come on," she said to me. "Let's show Sam how wrong he is."

I didn't budge, which was pretty easy since the sight of myself had more or less turned me to stone. "I told you. I'm not going out there. Not like this."

Lola groaned. "Oh, for heaven's sake, Ella. What does it matter? Nobody's going to know it's you, are they? That wig practically obliterates your face." She grabbed hold of my elbow and started tugging me toward the door. "And, anyway, you look great. I can practically hear the ukuleles playing."

I dug in my flip-flops.

"I don't look great. I look like a guy in drag pretending to be a hula dancer."

"Put on the glasses," ordered Lola. "I want Sam to get the full effect."

It took Sam a few seconds to recover from the full effect.

"Christ!" He sat up, wiping his eyes. If my mother had seen the state of my bed after Sam collapsed on it, he would really have had something to cry about. "I thought you were going to be the Swedish Chef and his assistant or something like that."

Lola kicked his foot. "Come on," she urged. "Admit it. You would never have known it was us in a million years."

"Two million." Sam winked. "But I would have noticed you. Especially Ella. She looks like an Easter basket with legs."

"Well, no one at the party's going to notice us," said Lola. "The Santinis will be too busy, and as far as anyone else is concerned, we're just the servants. No one ever looks at the servants."

"Maybe," Sam conceded. "I mean, the disguises are pretty good, but I still don't like it. And just for the record, I'm not really all that happy about staying here to baby-sit your mom. What am I supposed to do if she wakes up while you're gone?"

"She won't wake up," Lola promised. Altogether, Lola and I found three empty wine bottles. It was amazing my mother had been able to stand for as long as she had. "She's down for the count."

"And anyway," I added. "If she does wake up, the sight of you will make her pass out again."

"Great," said Sam. "That makes me feel a whole lot better."

19

Stalemate at Casa Santini

"Look," said Lola as we flew through the gates with the legend *Casa Santini* woven into the metalwork, "even the house is wearing a costume. It looks like the gym when it's decorated for a dance."

This wasn't really accurate: it looked like the White House decorated for a dance.

There were blue and white lights across the Santinis' roof and all along the circular drive, and blue and white balloons floating above the mailbox and the wrought-iron fence that keeps the riffraff out. Hanging from the porch was a large silk banner that said CARLA SANTINI— YOU KNOW SHE'S THE BEST.

"The sign's a nice touch," I said as we bucked to a stop. "At least no one will have any trouble finding the house."

Lola took the keys from the ignition and dropped them into the shoulder bag she'd borrowed from my mother. Then she pulled off her sneakers and put on the heels she'd also borrowed from my mother, which didn't fit well enough to drive in. Then she looked at her watch. "Seven on the dot. All systems go."

Lola figured that it was better to be late than on time. If we'd arrived at six, as promised, Carla and her mother would have wanted to talk to us. But by now, reasoned Lola, they'd both be too busy getting ready to come sniffing around.

Lola opened the driver's door and carefully lowered herself to the ground, the chopsticks she'd stuck in her wig tilting dangerously. "Come on. You and I are about to give the performance of a lifetime."

Gathering my portable lawn around me, I climbed out of the passenger seat. "Is that before we get caught, or after?"

"Scoff all you want," said Lola. "But I have a feeling about tonight. I think it's going to be one to remember."

"Isn't that what they said about the night the *Titanic* went down?"

Lola headed toward the rear of the car. She was wobbling in a pretty alarming way. Plastic grass swaying, I trotted after her.

"Are you supposed to be impersonating my mother, or are you about to kill yourself on those shoes?" I hissed.

She opened the back. "I just haven't quite got the hang of them yet."

"Well, try not to fall over. Here comes Maria Jesús."

Maria Jesús, the Santinis' maid, must have been waiting for us. She came scuttling down the front path, calling,

"Mrs. Gerard! Mrs. Gerard! I'll help you with the food!" Maria Jesús was dressed as a maid.

"It might have been more appropriate if she were dressed as a person," muttered Lola.

Mrs. Santini and Carla, said Maria Jesús, were putting on clothes.

"Well, thank God for that," mumbled Lola.

We went in through the back. Tradesmen's entrance.

"You see?" whispered Lola. "Didn't I tell you? We're just the hired help."

Lola caught her breath as we came around the side of the house and stumbled into a bush. "Look at this, will you? You'd think she was running for president of the country, not president of Dellwood High."

Even I, who had been to more than enough Carla Santini parties in my time to know what they were like, was impressed.

What the Santinis call their "backyard" most other people would call a park. It was divided into two sections. The section nearest the house held the patio, the swimming pool, the tennis court, and Mrs. Santini's Japanese rock garden, complete with pond, wooden bridge, and a small shed for the man who actually did the work, Maria Jesús' husband, Joachim. Behind that—separated by a high hedge with an archway cut in it—was the garden proper (flowers, a lawn that put the golf course to shame, and a freestanding deck with a roof). Both sections were strung with dozens more blue and white lights and balloons. Inflatable globes bobbed in the pool and the pond.

Two enormous buffet tables—one for the food and one for the drinks—stood against the kitchen wall. The band was setting up on the deck at the back of the garden, where there was enough room for the whole town of Dellwood to dance.

"Maybe we should've poisoned the food after all," I whispered. "Nobody's going to vote for us after this."

Maria Jesús was already at the patio doors. "Come, come!" she begged. "Miss Carla has been worried."

"You see?" said Lola. "There's always some good news."

Maria Jesus showed us where everything was—the stove, the oven, the microwave, and the box of tiny flags of all nations to be stuck into the platters of crab cakes and samosas—and then she bustled off to finish laying the buffet table.

"What'd I tell you?" Lola whispered as the glass doors closed on Maria Jesús. "This is going to be easier than filling a taco shell. All we have to do is get this stuff onto serving dishes and we're home free."

But any child of Aeschylus would ask you, *What is home? What is free?* And that child would be right.

On cue as ever, Carla Santini burst through the kitchen door. She looked the same as always, except that she was wearing a little more makeup than usual and a bathrobe.

"Mrs. Gerard!" Carla's voice was shrill with relief. "I've been sooo worried about you. I thought something must have happened."

145

I bent over one of our boxes and started removing containers.

Lola pulled a fan out of the sleeve of her kimono and ducked behind it. "Oh, Carla, honey. I'm terribly sorry we're so late." I assumed from the way she was speaking that geishas have childish, lilting voices. "I'm afraid we had a little disaster with the satay."

"Oh, that doesn't matter." Carla had crossed the kitchen by now and was near enough to Lola to melt her makeup with her breath. "As long as *you're* all right . . ."

Lola's fan was moving between them as fast as a hummingbird's wings. "I'm fine . . . just fine . . ."

"Are you sure you don't have a headache?" Carla peered as closely as she could without getting poked in the eye. "Your face looks a little puffy."

Lola slapped her playfully on the head with the fan. "Hee-hee-hee . . . ," she tittered. "That's from sampling too much of my own cooking, that's what that is."

Carla had withstood the playful slap all right, but she jumped back as Lola's fan grazed her nose.

Lola spun around to face the sink and started washing her hands.

"You look great as a geisha," said Carla. Now she was staring at Lola's backside, probably wondering if it was the cummerbund that made it look larger than she remembered, or if my mother really had put on weight in the last few days.

I tried to distract Carla as best I could without actually drawing attention to myself. "Microwave?" I croaked.

Carla didn't even glance my way. She waved one hand toward the microwave and said to Lola, "How about a glass of wine, Mrs. Gerard? My parents are having a few people over, too, you know, so there's plenty of chardonnay in the fridge."

I dropped the samosas.

"Hee-hee-hee," giggled the geisha at the sink. "I never drink while I'm working."

"Really?" I couldn't see Carla's face, but her voice was smiling slyly. "I'm sure you were having a glass of wine the other day when I stopped by."

The water kept running. Lola was washing her hands so thoroughly you'd have thought she was going to operate on the food, not just heat it up. "That was at home. This is professional."

"Oh," Carla purred. "I understand . . ." She leaned a little closer and sniffed. "Is that a new perfume, Mrs. Gerard?"

Perfume! We'd forgotten about the perfume. My mother always wore Opium.

"Hee-hee-hee," tittered the humble geisha. "I thought it was time for a change."

"I see," murmured Carla. The way she was staring at Lola, I was afraid she did see; straight through the heavy makeup to the youthful skin underneath. I was about to drop the samosas again—this time on Carla—when another character in our little drama entered, stage right.

Mrs. Santini thundered through the door. Mrs. Santini's idea of looking French was Marie Antoinette.

147

"What are you doing now, Carla?" She sounded as though she was always finding Carla in unlikely places, doing dumb things. "Look at you. The guests will be arriving any minute, and you're not even dressed."

I ducked behind the refrigerator.

Mrs. Santini noticed the geisha with the incredibly clean hands and her voice did a 180-degree turn.

"Marilyn!" You could tell where Carla learned to gush. "I didn't hear you drive up. Do you have everything you need? Did Maria Jesús show you where everything is? Carla wasn't bothering you, was she?"

"Oh, yes, yes . . . No, of course not."

The social niceties taken care of, Mrs. Santini turned back to her daughter. "We'd better leave Marilyn and Mrs. Wallace in peace, honey." She laughed. It was eerie how much like her Carla was. You'd think she'd been cloned. "And you'd better finish getting dressed . . ."

Lola didn't turn the taps off till they were safely out of the room.

"Alone at last," breathed Lola.

"Let's do this as fast as we can." My heart was pounding and my palms were damp. "I just want to get out of here before anybody else shows up."

We unpacked everything in under five minutes, and then we started sticking things into the oven and the microwave.

I began to breathe almost normally.

"You worry too much," said Lola. "You have to learn to relax. Everything's under control."

At which moment Mr. Santini marched into the kitchen, dressed as a Cossack with an authentic glass of vodka in his hand.

"Marilyn!" cried Mr. Santini. He slammed down his glass and threw his arms around Lola in what I assumed was a Russian bear hug. "Forget the food! You look good enough to eat!" He inhaled deeply. "You've changed your perfume, haven't you? You smell delicious."

Even Lola was momentarily caught by surprise. It was just as well he was holding her, or she probably would have toppled.

"Mis—" she began, but caught herself in time. "Anthony! Hee-hee-hee . . ." Smiling all the while, she elegantly disentangled herself by elbowing Mr. Santini in the stomach. She flicked her fan in front of her face and tittered some more. "It's bad luck to see the cook before the party," she said in her new soft, singsong voice.

Mr. Santini was charmed. He stood there, grinning at her soupily. I started to wonder if maybe my mother's wasn't the only drinking problem in Woodford.

"That's the bride before the wedding," said Mr. Santini. He leaned closer. He was wearing hunting boots, but he was wobbling, too. "You know," he said, his voice low but still loud enough to be heard by the help, "I've always been attracted to Japanese women."

"Why, Tony!" Lola whacked him playfully in the chest with her fan. "What will Mrs. Wallace think?"

Maybe Mr. Santini didn't believe that Mrs. Wallace could think. Like his only child, he didn't so much as glance my way.

"You know, you've never called me Tony before." If his smile got any soupier, he was going to drown them both.

From behind her fan, Lola said, "That's because you've never bothered me when I'm trying to work before. Hee-hee-hee." She ducked to look in the oven.

Mr. Santini stared down at the top of her wig. He seemed fascinated by the chopsticks. "You know, I'd really like to have a dance with you later on," he drawled.

Lola stood up so quickly that Mr. Santini had to jump back to avoid being hit in the teeth.

"Later," Lola tittered. She fluttered her fan between them, and, holding on to the counter, gave him a shove. "Now get out of this kitchen before I change my mind."

"But you do promise you'll have a dance?" insisted Mr. Santini. "Later?"

This turned out to be Mrs. Santini's second cue of the night.

"Oh, there you are, darling." Only Mrs. Santini's mouth was smiling. She looked like a Marie Antoinette who'd just heard about the Revolution. "The Derrings and the Bartons have just arrived. Don't you think you should be out there to greet them?"

It sounded like a question, but Mr. Santini knew a threat when he heard one. He blinked a couple of times and then he hopped to it.

"I'm on my way, darling," purred Mr. Santini. "Just thought I'd make sure the cook was all right."

"And is she?"

If Mr. Santini heard the sourness in her voice, he pretended that he hadn't. "She's fine." He picked up his glass and glided past his wife, winking at my mother over her shoulder.

"I'm sorry about that. . . ." Mrs. Santini's mouth was still smiling. "I guess he's excited . . . you know, with the rally and everything . . . Did I tell you he's buying Carla a new car if she wins? He's wound up like a kid at Christmas. You know how he loves to spoil her."

Lola fluttered her fan. "Oh, yes, I know. And he's done a wonderful job."

I ducked behind the door of the microwave.

"Anyway, I am sorry if he was getting underfoot."

"Oh, please, Mela, there's nothing to be sorry for . . . You just go and enjoy yourself."

Mrs. Santini finally gave up on the smile. "As if I ever could," she said. And with that she swept back out of the room.

Lola was rolling her eyes. "What a family." She said it with feeling. "Maybe we should stick around. I bet we could dig up something interesting about the Santinis if we tried." She put on a deep voice and winked like Mr. Santini. "Maybe we wouldn't have to try too hard."

By ten o'clock there must have been over two hundred people in the backyard. And there, right in the middle—like a jewel in a crown—was Carla Santini. Carla had topped everyone by coming as Miss New Jersey, in the evening-gown competition. At least half a dozen times I'd caught her looking suspiciously toward the kitchen, but (fortunately) she was always mobbed by adoring fans and though she looked like she wanted to, she couldn't come back in without bringing the varsity cheerleading squad with her.

"Well, Tonto, it looks like our job here is done," said Lola as the first of the fireworks lit up the sky. "It's time to ride back into the sunset."

Personally, I wouldn't have minded riding back into a blizzard as long as we got out of there. Carla wasn't the only one who was keeping an eye on us. Not only did Mr. Santini wave every time Lola looked outside, but it seemed to me that Marie Antoinette was paying a lot more attention to the kitchen than you'd expect from a queen.

"Great." I handed her a crate of empty containers. "You can take this and go saddle up the horses while I finish packing."

"Hi, ho, Silver!" Lola laughed.

"Marilyn!" Mr. Santini suddenly lunged into the kitchen. His Cossack hat was slightly askew, but he was still carrying a glass of vodka—though it was pretty obvious that it wasn't the same one. "Don't tell me you're

152

leaving. You can't leave yet. We haven't had our dance."
He gripped her wrist with his free hand.

Lola went into her giggling routine. "Oh, Anthony, I can't. I have to load the car."

"Let the hula girl do it," cried Mr. Santini, yanking her back through the patio doors. "You promised me a dance."

The hula girl finished packing up our things but decided not to wait in the car. How long could a dance take? I might as well wait inside. I poured myself a glass of soda and stood at the patio doors, watching the fireworks.

I can look at stars for hours, but after a few minutes, the fascination of the Santinis' pyrotechnic display kind of faded and I returned my gaze to the crowd behind the house. I couldn't see any Cossacks or geishas in the first section of the yard. My first instinct was to panic. Where were they? Had Mr. Santini realized it wasn't Marilyn Gerard he was dancing with? Worse still, had Carla or Mrs. Santini? I told myself to calm down. I told myself the Cossack and the geisha must be farther back, by the bandstand. The voice of panic, however, was still shrieking in my head. It wanted to know how Lola could get all the way to the back of the yard on grass in my mother's shoes.

I stepped onto the patio for a better look, straining to see over the heads of the crowd. Carla Santini stared back at me.

I ignored her and moved from the patio to the swimming pool for a better view. It was no use. The Santinis aren't quite feudal lords who could ride for a day and never leave their own land, but they were close enough for me. Still aware of the eyes of Carla Santini tracking me like a radar, I strolled on, as nonchalant and casual as someone who looks like an escapee from an amateur production of *South Pacific* can. I saw a lot of people I knew, of course. Football players dressed as cowboys and soldiers. Cheerleaders dressed as flamenco dancers and harem girls. Mr. Mazzucci, the manager of my father's bank, in his usual dark suit and a Winston Churchill mask. But I didn't see Lola or Mr. Santini.

I blame the various stresses of the day for the fact that it was only when I finally got within real sight of the bandstand that I realized the music had stopped.

How could you dance if there wasn't any music?

I squinted through the smoke-filled air. As far as I could tell, the answer to the question of dancing without music was that, in fact, you couldn't. The giggling geisha and the swaying Cossack were nowhere in sight.

As I rustled back the way I'd come, I caught Carla out of the corner of my eye. She was smiling and laughing at something the varsity star quarterback in the Sioux war bonnet was saying to her, but she was still watching me. I sailed past her on the other side of the yard and headed toward the side of the house. Maybe Mr. Santini, who by now must have consumed enough vodka to paralyze half the Russian army, had ducked down there to pass out in private and Lola had followed to make sure he was all right.

There were a couple of boys smoking behind the rhododendrons. I pretended I didn't see them, either. I finally stopped when I reached the front of the garage. I thought I heard voices coming from one of the rooms at the front of the house, but I was too preoccupied with wondering what to do next to pay any attention. I can see now that I should either have gone back inside or should have marched right across the lawn and continued my search up the other side of the house, but I didn't. I just stood there, wondering if I could have missed them in the backyard. Had I checked the tennis court? Did I thoroughly examine the throng around the buffet tables? Could I swear they weren't in the mob by the pool? I hadn't, I didn't, and I couldn't. I moaned out loud. "Please, Lola . . . ," I hissed into the darkness. "I really want to go home."

A sweet, kind voice—like the voice of an angel answering my prayers—spoke behind me.

"Do you need some help?" it asked.

But it wasn't an angel. My life had become a Greek drama, not a Christmas play. It was the voice of Carla Santini.

I was like Lot's wife: I knew what would happen if I turned around, but I turned around anyway.

Carla was wearing a delicate tiara and a regal smile. "Do you have a problem, Ella? Or are you lost?"

She must have followed me out of the backyard. I could tell from the expression on her face that there was no use in pretending to be Mrs. Wallace. I was busted. And I could also tell from the expression on Carla's face that she had a pretty good idea of what was going on. By Monday morning our community, our town, the school, and probably most of the glorious state of New Jersey would know what Carla guessed—and probably a lot more.

I mustered together as much dignity and cool as I could. "No, no problem. I was just about to leave."

Carla's smile was ten times brighter than a Roman candle, and ten times more dangerous. "Are you sure?"

Was I sure? Was I sure about what?

"Because I was thinking," said Carla. "I mean, you must have an awful lot on your plate already—you know, with your mother's drinking problem and everything. . . ." She let her words hang in the air for a few seconds like a nuclear cloud; her look hung on me. "So, I was thinking . . . if you wanted to drop from the race . . ."

Maybe Carla will run for president of the country someday. All I had to do was drop out of the election and she'd keep her big mouth shut.

I didn't know what to do. My mother's whole life revolved around our community. Considering how badly she seemed to cope with success, what would happen to her if that was taken away from her, too? Especially the way things were between her and my father.

Carla's not just a witch, she's a mind reader as well. "Think about it, Ella. Your mother obviously needs a lot of support right now, not conflict."

156

I cleared my throat.

Her smile moved from Roman candle to nuclear proportions. "Is that a yes?"

It was. I was going to say yes. It didn't seem like I had a choice.

And then the front door opened and someone screamed, "Are you nuts? Get away from me, you lech!"

Carla and I both looked over as Lola Cep stalked out of the house, her wig askew and my mother's shoes in her hands.

Lola stopped on the porch and turned back to the opened door. "Don't think this is the last you're going to hear of this, Mr. Anthony Santini!" she roared. "Because it isn't. I'm going to tell your wife what you suggested. I'm going to tell your friends. I'm going to make sure that everyone knows exactly what kind of man you are."

"Ella?" said Carla.

I turned to look at her; she was already looking at me.

And in that instant, I made the first political deal of my life. Carla would keep her mouth shut about my mother, and in return I'd make sure that Lola kept her mouth shut about Carla's dad.

I smiled. "Well," I said. "Thanks for the great party, Carla. I guess Lola and I will be going now."

20

Trust in the Greeks

My mother was in one of her good moods on Sunday morning. She glided around the kitchen, singing along to the radio as though Saturday had never happened. She didn't even seem to have a hangover, which was pretty unfair. I hadn't had anything stronger than soda and I felt like hell.

And for about a second, when I came into the kitchen and saw her smiling, I was tempted to act like yesterday had never happened, too. Just like I always did. But then she asked me what I wanted for breakfast, and instead of saying just some really strong coffee, I said, "Mom, we have to talk."

I sounded like someone in a movie, and probably not a good one.

My mother thought so, too. She laughed.

"Really," I said. "About yesterday."

She immediately started apologizing. She wanted to thank me for getting the food over to the Santinis. She didn't know what she would have done without me. I said Lola and Sam helped, and she didn't even flinch when she said to thank them, too.

"I know it was silly," my mother told me, "but I thought I'd have a little wine while I was cooking, and it went right to my head." She thought she'd lie down for a few minutes, and the next thing she knew it was morning.

I poured myself a coffee and leaned against the sideboard. "That's not what happened."

Her smile was a little nervous. "Of course that's what happened." She opened the refrigerator and started looking for something at the back. "All I can say is, thank God I finished the cooking. At least that's something."

I picked up my cup. "But not very much."

She came out of the refrigerator with a jar of homemade jam. "Meaning?"

"Meaning we really have to talk. Now."

At first she tried to stick to her story about not feeling well. That was all she remembered. She didn't remember trashing the kitchen. She didn't remember passing out in Lola's arms. She obviously didn't know that, despite my and Lola's best efforts, Carla knew about her drinking problem. So I told her.

My mother's face went pink. "Carla?"

"It's all right," I said. "She's not going to tell anybody."

"I should think not," said my mother. "The way Anthony drinks."

But I didn't want to talk about anybody else's drinking habits right then. "And what about the letter from Dad

159

and wanting to go to London? Are you saying you don't remember that, either?"

For a few seconds she didn't say anything. She just stared back at me, like a rabbit in the headlights. And then she started to cry.

It wasn't the longest conversation I'd ever had. The longest conversation I'd ever had was with Lola, and it clocked in at over six hours. But it was the longest conversation I'd ever had with my mother or anyone else. Especially with my mother.

We talked about her and my father for hours. Last night she'd wanted to confront him, but now she wasn't sure what she wanted to do. After all, it wasn't as if he was the only one who was unhappy.

Eventually, she even started to come around to the idea that a break from each other wasn't such a bad thing. "You know, I've never lived on my own except in college and then I always had a roommate," said my mother.

I was tempted to tell her that Lola Cep says you have to live by yourself in order to have real personal growth and know who you are, but I thought better of it. Instead I said, "Well, you don't really have anything to lose, do you?"

"I guess not." My mother sighed. "It's not as if things could get any worse, is it?"

I decided not to say anything about that, either.

But it was harder to get her to talk about the drinking. Yes, she drank too much sometimes, but she didn't consider it a problem. "I don't think I have to check into the Betty Ford Center just yet," joked my mother.

I didn't smile. "But you do have to get help."

She promised she would.

I said that was excellent, because there was an AA meeting on Monday nights in the next town from Dellwood and I was going to drive her there myself. She was so surprised by that, that she didn't even ask me how I knew. Which was just as well. I figured she'd be even less happy about going if she found out Sam's aunt went there.

By the time the phone started ringing, we were actually laughing about what a sight Lola and I must have been, dressed up as her and Mrs. Wallace.

We looked at each other, but neither of us made a move to answer the phone.

My father's voice came at us from the answering machine. It was raining in London.

"Good God," I muttered. "He remembered the number."

My mother's head swung back and forth from the machine to me.

This was ridiculous. How was she ever going to sort out her life if she couldn't even pick up the phone without being told to?

My mother turned back to the machine. My father was trying to figure out what his phone number in London was when she took a deep breath and reached for the receiver.

"Robert?" She took another deep breath. "I'm glad you called." She glanced at me over her shoulder. "We really have to talk."

Getting Marilyn Gerard to talk about her drinking problem was difficult, but not as difficult as convincing Lola Cep to keep her mouth shut about Mr. Santini.

"Has the great Santini hypnotized you or something?" wailed Lola. "I would never've let you talk me out of telling Mrs. Santini last night in front of everybody if I'd known this was what you wanted me to do."

"I don't want you to do anything," I said patiently. "For once I want you to do absolutely nothing. Just keep your mouth shut and act like nothing happened."

Lola flung herself down on my bed, but I didn't even blink. She eyed me critically. "You could probably be certified for this, you know. You're totally out of your mind."

"That's the deal I made with Carla, Lo. We keep quiet about her father's interest in women he isn't married to, and she keeps quiet about my mother's fondness for white wine."

Lola moaned some more. "But this is the opportunity of a lifetime, Ella. Think of it: 'Top Lawyer Propositions Minor.' The papers will have a field day. The talk shows will be killing themselves to get me on."

And the Santinis would simply be killing each other.

"Let's be fair here," I argued. "Mr. Santini didn't know he was propositioning a minor."

162

"And what difference does that make?" I wasn't sure which actor she was doing now, but it was someone very good at disdain. "He thought he was hitting on his wife's best friend."

"There is a difference."

"Yeah," said Lola. "One's against the law."

"Which is another reason why you're not going to say anything." I gave her my most stern look. "It'd be a horrible thing to do. Even Mr. Santini doesn't deserve that."

Bracelets clinked and eyes rolled. "You can't really believe that. We are talking about the man who spawned Carla Santini."

"It was an honest mistake."

"You mean it was a *drunken* mistake."

"Exactly. He'd had a lot of vodka."

Lola gazed back, unblinking.

"He was totally taken in by your acting. How was he to know the truth?"

Lola looked a little smug at the mention of her acting, but she held her ground. "That's all beside the point. The fact remains that he should've kept his hands off the geisha, no matter who she was." She looked like she'd just bit into something disgusting. I knew that look. It meant she was willing to compromise. "Tell you what. What if I just drop some discreet hints?"

But I held my ground, too. "The most important fact is that I made a deal with Carla. I have no intention of going back on my promise."

Lola howled contemptuously. "And you don't think she does?" She jumped to her feet, hands flailing the air. "You're deluding yourself on a major scale, Ella, if you think Carla Santini's going to keep her promise. And even if she doesn't say anything before the election, she'll say plenty as soon as it's over. You can bet your mom's last friend on that."

But now that I was starting to be me, losing myself again seemed a lot worse than my mother losing her last golf partner. "I'm not going back on my principles just because it's possible that Carla doesn't have any. I'd be no better than she is then."

Lola stared at me for a second. She wasn't doing anyone now except Lola. I could tell that this time I had her. She didn't want me to lose me, either. And then she threw up her arms, imploring the gods. "Is life ironic, or what?" she wailed. "Of all the political candidates in the world, I have to get the one with principles." She looked back at me. "What about after the election, Ella? It'll be seconds, not minutes, before the whole of Woodford knows about your mother."

"Then it'll be nanoseconds before the whole of Woodford knows about her dad."

I have principles, but I don't believe in being inflexible.

There was an almost carnival atmosphere on campus that final week of the campaign.

Carla leapt into the last days before the election like someone who's just walked miles across the desert and

164

then jumped into a pool. High as Jupiter on the success of her rally, she raced around on fast-forward, keeping the buzz alive. Everywhere you looked, there she was: smiling, or posing, or shaking some poor fool's hand.

She'd given up the balloons because Morty and his friends never tired of popping them, but in their place she'd had herself wired for sound. Wherever she went, her campaign song ("Simply the Best," naturally) followed.

Even Morty was almost animated as the election drew to an end. He strode through the corridors, nodding, grinning, and giving practically every person he passed the thumbs-up. I had the distinct impression from the number of people who responded that no one thought he worked in the office anymore.

It was not, however, a carnival atmosphere in which I took part. I was too nervous.

"It's just preelection jitters," Lola assured me as we walked to lunch on Monday. "Everybody gets them. Kennedy got them. Franklin Roosevelt got them. Even Reagan got them, and he was asleep most of the time."

"Really?" I was willing to be convinced.

"Really. It's like stage fright, Ella. It's just the adrenaline kicking in. It's a good sign."

If that was true, I'd really hate to experience a bad sign.

I went to find a table while Lola joined the lunch line.

There were two empty seats at the table in the far corner. I headed for that.

I was opening my lunch box when the one political candidate in the history of the world who knew nothing about preelection jitters suddenly sat down beside me.

I jumped.

"Gloriana, Ella," said Carla, demonstrating the empathy and concern that had earned her a Good Citizen Award from the Dellwood Chamber of Commerce. "You're a bundle of nerves."

"I didn't hear you coming." I plonked my Thermos on the table. "You turned off your sound system."

Carla's smile brought the temperature down. "How's your mom, Ella? Feeling better?"

"She's feeling great." I smiled back. "How's your dad?"

Carla sat down next to me. "I wanted to have a quick word with you alone."

Since there were over a hundred people in the cafeteria at the time, I assumed that "alone" meant without Lola.

I figured she was worried that Lola wouldn't keep her mouth shut.

"If it's Lola—"

"It's not Lola." She gave me one of her biggest smiles. "It's the debate."

"The debate?"

Carla laughed. "Don't tell me you forgot about the debate."

"Of course not."

"Well, that's good." Carla turned up the wattage on her smile. It was enough to make the blind see. "I'm really looking forward to it."

Our corner of the cafeteria vibrated with her laughter. "I haven't had a real debate since I won the state championship in junior high. Remember?"

I did now.

"So what was it you wanted to talk about?" I asked. Cautiously.

"I just didn't want you to be laboring under an illusion, that's all," said the girl with a heart as big as Texas. "You know. Because of our . . . our little agreement."

And what illusion would that be?

"I just want to make sure it's clear that our arrangement doesn't affect the debate," continued Carla. "I'm not going to wear gloves because of that. That's a separate issue." She waggled her fingers in my direction. Her nails were black this week, to match her heart.

"Well, I definitely wouldn't want you to do that," I said.

"Great." Carla dredged up a look of sympathy. "It's just that I know debating's not really your thing, Ella. I wanted you to be prepared."

I tried to look humbled by her consideration. "How kind of you."

"There's no need to get sarcastic." She arched one eyebrow. "I mean, after what happened in English that time—"

Unlike some of us, Carla Santini forgets nothing.

"That was a long time ago."

"Hmm . . . ," said Carla. "I just wouldn't want you to humiliate yourself again like that." People around me shielded their eyes from the blinding light of her smile. "In front of the whole school."

I smiled back. "Then that makes two of us, doesn't it?" I asked.

The Greeks were back in my life, but this time I knew what was going to go wrong.

"You'd think you'd have developed a more philosophical attitude by now," said Lola as we walked toward the cafeteria on Wednesday. "She's just trying to scare you."

"And it's worked. My palms are sweating already and the debate's not until tomorrow."

Lola laughed. "Oh, please . . . let's not overlook the fact that you've been coached by the best. You know your spiel inside out. Besides, I'll be right there—front row, center—for moral support. And to whisper the answers if you do dry up." She gave me a hug. "Trust me, Ella. You're going to be great."

Sam, however, recognized the sincerity in my abject terror. "Tell you what," said Sam. "If you really are that nervous, maybe you should brief me before the debate." He gave me a look. "You know, in case something happens and I have to take over."

Lola's jewelry clanged and banged and rattled. "What do you mean, 'in case something happens'? Ella's not going to be struck by lightning, Sam. Get real, will you? What could happen?"

"Well," said that familiar voice of strychnine laced with saccharine, "she *could* freeze up."

We all turned around. Carla and Alma had materialized behind us, the way evil specters do.

"Don't hold your breath," said Lola. She matched the famous Santini smile tooth for tooth. "On second thoughts, do. I'm sure we could squeeze your funeral into our schedule after the election."

Carla wasn't even looking at Lola. Carla only had eyes for me. "You're very lucky, aren't you?" purred Carla. "You always get saved by the cavalry." She blitzed me with another smile. "Let's just hope your luck doesn't run out."

21

The Great Debate

All things considered, I woke up in a pretty positive frame of mind on Thursday morning. I was determined not to worry. Lola was right; I had been well coached. And I'd stayed up till one in the morning, memorizing my introductory speech, so I wouldn't have to read from my notes. And if something did go horribly wrong and I froze or went totally blank, I knew I could rely on Lola to stage some distraction. You know, faint or turn out the lights—something like that.

I took longer than usual to get ready on Thursday morning because I wanted to look my best. The debate was being held in a special assembly right after home-room, so there wouldn't be any time to repair makeup or redo hair. I'd been planning to wear my blue A-line with the matching jacket, but when I looked at it in the cold morning light it looked so much like something Hillary Clinton would wear that I put it back in the closet. I knew Lola was wearing her purple camouflage pants and the Free Tibet T-shirt her father brought her back from India, but my wardrobe didn't include any clothes that might be considered a declaration of war. I went for the dragon shirt Lola gave me and my black jeans. At least the shirt was red.

Lola always met me at the entrance to Woodford in the morning. If I was a little late, she'd chat with Fabio, the security guard. I was a little late that Thursday morning, but Fabio was alone in his booth.

I wasn't worried. Lola (being Lola) is late a lot more often than I am. It happens all the time.

Fabio looked up when the news on the radio finished. "Doesn't look like she's coming, does it?"

This wasn't unheard of, either. Not only does Lola take ages to get ready for anything more public than putting the garbage out, but her family is very prone to domestic crises. Things are always exploding, or breaking, or getting lost. I waited an hour and a half for her once because her sisters' gerbil got trapped under the floor.

"Doesn't she have a cell phone?" asked Fabio.

The answer to that was "no." Lola would sell one of the twins to get a cell phone, but her mother won't let her have one. She says it would be like giving a knife to a serial killer.

Fabio handed me his phone. "Call her from here. See what happened."

The answering machine was on.

"Maybe her mother gave her a ride," suggested Fabio.

"Yeah," I said. "She probably did."

But I was now officially starting to worry despite my resolution not to. I imagined dark, hooded figures standing along the side of the road, chanting in Greek, as I pedaled along.

"Don't be ridiculous," I told myself. "She'll be waiting at the bike rack."

It was Sam who was waiting at the bike rack.

"Where's Lola?" I called as I coasted to a stop.

Sam gave me one of his "Are you talking to me?" looks. "Isn't she supposed to be with you?"

"She didn't turn up at the gate."

"Well, you know Lola." Sam gave me a reassuring grin. "I'm sure there's an explanation." You'll notice he didn't say "logical explanation." "She wouldn't miss today for anything but a Broadway part."

And it would have to be a really good part.

"You're right," I said. "I'm getting myself worked up about nothing. Maybe she had a flat tire or something. She's probably on her way."

Sam took his cell phone out of his pocket. "Phone your mom. See if Lola called after you left."

Lola hadn't called.

The dark, hooded figures who had been lining the road all the way to school were now standing in front of the administration building, muttering to themselves.

"Maybe Karen gave her a lift," Sam suggested. I wasn't sure if he was trying to make me feel better, or himself. "She's probably already in homeroom."

Lola wasn't in homeroom.

Carla Santini was. She was wearing a dark green silk pants suit and a smile that could freeze gasoline.

"Where's Tweedledum?" she whispered as I passed her seat. "Don't tell me she's deserted you in your hour of need?"

I don't know if Sam heard her or not, but he picked his books back up from his desk. "Tell you what," he said into my ear. "I'll just go take a quick spin and look for her. You know, in case she did get a flat. I'll be right back."

If Carla Santini hadn't been watching us as if we were about to start sprouting flowers, I would have begged him not to leave me. But I could feel Carla's eyes on us, so all I did was nod.

Mr. Geraldi looked up. "Was it something I said, Sam?" he asked. "Won't you change your mind and stay?"

"I left my gym stuff in the car. I'll be right back."

"Yeah, right . . . ," snorted Alma. "He won't be back till lunch."

Tina and Marcia giggled.

"Shhh . . . ," hissed Carla, swiveling her whole head around to glance at me. "Don't tease Ella. You know how nervous she is about the debate."

By the end of homeroom, I was so nervous I was practically hyperventilating. Not only was there no sign of Lola, but there was no sign of Sam, either.

I couldn't believe it! After all I'd done for her—lied, stolen, been arrested—the one time I really needed Lola, she wasn't around. And I wasn't even asking for any major sacrifices. All I wanted was a little moral support. Was that too much to ask? A little moral support, and someone to grab the mike if I fainted?

Where is she? I kept asking myself. *Where could she be?*

I feel like a fool saying it now, but not for the most infinitesimal fraction of a second was I worried that Lola might have been run over or anything like that. I know Lola has a lot of faults—she exaggerates, she's manipulative, she's a pathological liar—but a lack of loyalty is not one of them. And yet all I could think of right then was me.

Where is she? Where could she be? How could she do this to me?

By the time Morty, Carla, and I got to the auditorium, I was starting to shake.

Morty stood with me making chitchat while we waited behind the curtain for the sound check to be done.

Casual to the point of boredom, Carla lounged on one side of the stage. Every time she caught my eye, Carla would glance at her watch and give me a hopeless smile.

I peered through the curtains for the zillionth time. There was still no sign of Lola or Sam.

"Stop worrying," advised Morty. "They'll turn up. Lola wouldn't miss—"

"I know," I snapped. "Lola wouldn't miss this if she were dead."

Morty put a hand on my shoulder. "You have to calm down, Ella. Remember what happened that time you had to give a speech in English. You don't want to make yourself vomit again."

"Thanks," I said. "That really makes me feel better."

"I don't even see what the big deal is," Morty went on. "I mean, it doesn't really make any difference if she's here or not."

"It does to me." Now my voice was starting to shake.

Dr. Alsop clapped his hands and told us to get in our places. "Just two minutes to go," he announced.

He might as well have been announcing the time for my hanging.

"No Lola yet?" asked Carla as she took her seat. She turned to Morty, suddenly in conversational mode. "That's what happens when you rely on someone like Lola, isn't it?" said Carla. "She only thinks of herself."

"Which makes her different from whom?" asked Morty.

The lights went on, the curtains opened, and Dr. Alsop stepped up to the lectern.

My stomach lurched.

Dr. Alsop gave one of his "little" talks about the election and how energetic and passionate it had been. You could hear someone snoring in the middle of the auditorium.

Then he explained the format of the debate. Dr. Alsop would introduce each of the candidates in turn; and each of the candidates would give a brief speech setting out his or her basic platform. Then Dr. Alsop would read out questions submitted by the students, and each candidate would be given a turn to reply.

Dr. Alsop folded his hands in front of him in a final kind of way when he was done. "Anything anyone wants to ask?"

It was meant to be a rhetorical question, but someone at the back shouted out, "Yes. Is Carla having a victory party, too?"

Dr. Alsop was one of the few people who didn't laugh.

Carla was introduced first. As soon as Dr. Alsop spoke her name, some of her supporters started shouting and whistling. It sounded like the football team.

Dr. Alsop told them to settle down.

Carla wiped a tear from her eye for this unexpected and spontaneous demonstration of affection and said a few well-chosen words about her civic and environmental record, as well as her commitment to enjoying yourself and having fun.

"After all," said Carla, "it's not going to end world hunger if you don't buy yourself that double cheeseburger, is it?"

Morty was introduced next. Morty's supporters were more subtle than Carla's. They turned on tiny flashlights and hummed the song from some computer game. Morty compared high school to the cosmos. I stopped listening when he started talking about quantum mechanics, and I suspect that everyone else did, too.

And then it was my turn.

"I saw her," Morty whispered as we passed. "Toward the back."

No one clapped or whistled or flashed their lights for me.

I hung on to the lectern and stared out at the sea of people in front of me. Blindly. Morty was lying; there was no way he could have seen Lola in the glare from the stage lights. On the other hand, I told myself, that didn't mean she wasn't out there. Maybe she was pinned against a wall in back and couldn't wave. Pinned against the wall and gagged.

She is there . . . She is there . . . She is there . . . I silently chanted. *She is there . . . She is there . . . She is there . . . Way, way at the back with a handkerchief stuffed in her mouth.*

Feeling as though I might possibly be able to speak and breathe at the same time, I cleared my throat. I took a deep breath and smiled into the blur of faces. I dropped my notes on the floor.

Someone indelicately giggled very softly behind me. It didn't sound like Morty.

It was Dr. Alsop who said, "Shhh."

Dr. Alsop helped me pick up my papers.

"Just take your time, Ella," he whispered. "You'll be fine."

I'd never wanted to believe anyone so much in my life.

I cleared my throat again, took another deep breath, and—gripping my notes like a life preserver—began to read my speech.

"Can't hear her!" screamed several people at once.

Dr. Alsop fluttered. "Could you speak up, please, Ella?" He gave me a fatherly smile.

I took yet another deep breath and tried again.

"Still can't hear her!" someone shouted.

"She hasn't said anything," shouted someone else.

Oh, how I wished I would faint.

Dr. Alsop scampered over and adjusted the microphone. "Try it now."

This time I yelled my entire speech, reading it without interruption, and without once looking up from my notes. I could tell from the rustlings and coughs that it wasn't exactly mesmerizing, but it was short.

Morty gave me the thumbs-up as I crumbled into the chair beside him.

Carla gave me a charitable smile. "You did really well," she whispered. Her smile became an entire soup kitchen. "At least you didn't throw up, right?"

"Ms. Santini!" Dr. Alsop rapped on the edge of the lectern. "Why don't you start us off?"

The first question came completely out of the blue.

"'What is your position on student demonstrations?'" read Dr. Alsop.

I was trying to get my notes back in order and looked up so sharply I nearly dropped them again.

"At Dellwood?" muttered Morty. "You'd be more likely to find a flock of demonstrating parrots."

Carla stood up. "In my opinion, the students of Dellwood High demonstrate every day. They demonstrate their intelligence, their interest in the world, and their moral fiber in everything they do. That's the kind of demonstration I believe in." Carla sat down.

"Mr. Slinger?" prompted Dr. Alsop.

Mr. Slinger stood up.

"Of course I believe that students should demonstrate when there's a just cause. It's a democratic right. And, as we can't vote and adults rarely listen to us, it's the one we have a duty to exercise." Morty raised one arm in the air and twisted his fingers around each other in what I assumed was some kind of computer freak sign. "And don't forget!" Morty boomed. "In this technocratic age, hacking is a form of social protest, too!"

Morty's fellow freaks raised their flashlights and stamped their feet in appreciation of this insight.

Dr. Alsop rapped once more. "That's enough, now. Settle down." He smiled at me. "Ms. Gerard?"

I stood up and looked at the microphone. I didn't know what to say. Morty wasn't the only one who didn't associate student unrest with Dellwood High. He gave me a nudge.

"Put your head down if you're feeling nauseous," whispered Carla.

I went on automatic pilot; I gave an answer I knew. "Yes," I said, "I believe in student demonstrations." Even to me I sounded like the android in a bad science fiction movie. "I think that we should demonstrate our understanding of the world by becoming more involved in our community."

"There's actually a question here that's relevant to that," said Dr. Alsop. "Why don't we take it next?" He flipped through his cards. "'If we're to be more involved with the rest of the world, does this mean that any money we raise should be given to charity?'" he read.

The Carla Santini fan club cheered when Carla said that she thought charity should begin at home.

Morty pointed out that merely making a donation to a worthy cause isn't the same as being involved.

Carla patted my knee. "Your turn."

Trying to sound as human as possible, I said that if the student body decided it wanted to support a charity, then it should raise funds specifically for that—so that they weren't just giving money, they were doing something as well.

The next few questions were reassuringly predictable ones about the cafeteria menu, the dress code, and extracurricular activities. I got through without too much torture.

I won't say I started to relax, but I started to think about relaxing. My heart was now beating at a normal rate, and my temperature had gone back up to 98.6 degrees. It looked as though I was going to live through this after all.

It's a little difficult to explain what happened next. It all went pretty fast.

Dr. Alsop was tossing the questions and we were each taking a turn to answer them in a mature and civilized manner when suddenly Carla Santini said, "You know, that's a very interesting question, Dr. Alsop. I'd like to ask Ella what she thinks about counseling for students with special problems—I mean, since her mother's an alcoholic and everything."

"Uh-oh," said Morty.

The only other sound for about two full seconds was Dr. Alsop trying to breathe.

I looked straight into Carla Santini's eyes, green today to match her suit. "Poor Ella" said her smile. "You're about to become road kill."

And that's when I realized. *Oh, my God . . .* I thought. *How could I be so blind?* That was why Lola wasn't there. Because Carla had made sure that she wasn't. Carla wouldn't dare attack me like that if Lola were there, because she knew Lola would retaliate. And she knew that I wouldn't. She knew I'd crumble completely and sit helplessly by while she humiliated me in front of the entire school. With a little bit of luck I might even throw up—or at least cry. That would really make her day.

You can't . . . You can't . . . You can't . . . You can't . . . Lola was right; that was what I always said. It was what I always felt. It was what I was feeling now. *You can't do this . . . You can't do that . . . Obey all rules and always be polite.*

But as I looked into the perfect face of Carla Santini, something inside of me snapped into place. What I couldn't do was let her get away with this; that was what I really couldn't do.

I stood up at the microphone, shaking but eerily calm. I turned to Carla with the cool smile of true loathing.

"I'm glad you raised that question, Carla." I couldn't have sounded sweeter. "I know that most of us here in Dellwood are very lucky. Luckier than a lot of people. We have every advantage our society offers. We take for granted a lot of things that other people consider luxuries. A disaster is if the car won't start or the outfit we wanted to wear hasn't come back from the cleaner's. But that doesn't mean that our lives are really as perfect as they seem." I moved a little closer to the microphone, gently edging Carla out of the way. "All of us have problems that we have to deal with, even the luckiest among us." I glanced over at Carla. "The veneer of perfection can hide a lot of horrors." I turned back to the audience. "I'm sure that my mother isn't the only adult in Dellwood with a drinking problem." A few sniggers rippled through the audience. "Just as I'm sure that a lot of us have to deal with other things that are even worse." I picked a blur in the middle of the auditorium and stared straight at it. "Most of us deal with our problems by pretending that they don't exist. So instead of getting better, they get worse and worse. That's why I feel it's important that there is somewhere where we can discuss them and receive, if not solutions, at least support. It's only by openly facing things that we can begin to make our lives really perfect."

If I'd been in a movie, that would have been the moment when the entire student body of Dellwood High School stood up, applauding, and an angel won his wings.

But I wasn't, of course. And angels in Dellwood are thin on the ground.

Carla was on me as soon as the last word was out of my mouth.

"Oh, listen to you . . . ," she crowed. "I'm surprised you don't have violins playing in the background." She rolled her eyes at Alma in the front row. "It's typical, isn't it, Ella, that you want everyone to feel sorry for you, instead of acting responsibly and solving your problems yourself."

Sixteen years of reticence and good breeding beat a hasty retreat. "Oh, that's pretty rich," I said. I wasn't shaking anymore. "Coming from you."

"And just what do you mean by that?"

There was a popping sound and the mike went dead.

"Sound!" shouted several voices at once. "Sound!"

Neither Carla nor I gave a hair clip about sound.

"I'll tell you exactly what I mean," I answered.

It was downhill after that.

Dr. Alsop eventually stepped in and more or less literally pulled us apart.

"Ladies!" he shouted. "Ladies, please! This is a little more energy and passion than is really necessary!"

Carla and I kept right on.

Dr. Alsop started flapping his arms. "Close the curtains!" he ordered. "Close the curtains!"

Somebody turned out the lights.

That's when the audience stood up and cheered.

22

And the Winner Is . . .

After the sound and the lights came back on, Dr. Alsop quieted everyone down and made one of his impromptu speeches. Amazingly enough, he wasn't really angry over what happened; just a bit overwhelmed.

Dr. Alsop claimed our election was the most interesting, vital, and truest in spirit to American democracy of any that he'd seen in his many long years as a professional educator. Happy that all of his education and hard work had finally paid off, he beamed at us. "This is the most enthusiasm the Dellwood High student body has ever shown in their own government," he concluded, "and I'm proud of every one of you."

There was more clapping and cheering at that, and then Dr. Alsop made Morty, Carla, and me shake hands and wish each other luck. Like boxers.

"And come out fighting," Morty whispered as I shook Carla's hand.

"May the best candidate win!" cried Dr. Alsop.

Alma, Tina, and Marcia started to chant. "You know she's the best! You know she's the best!"

"Oh, I plan to," purred Carla.

Only the three of us on the stage with Carla heard her; and only Dr. Alsop thought she was making a joke.

As Carla strode down the stairs at the front in what can only be described as a triumphant procession of one, the Santini satellites all gathered around her.

I looked over at Morty. "You think she already won and nobody told us?"

"Well, she seems to think so." Morty sighed. "Maybe I shouldn't've pulled the plug on the mike. I was trying to stop her from blabbing your private stuff all over the school, but it looks like I protected her from publicly revealing her darker side."

"You did your best." Together we walked down the stairs after Carla.

"So did you," said Morty. "You were fantastic. I wish I had a picture of Carla's face when you were giving your perfect life speech. I'd have it framed and hang it in the office."

To tell the truth, I was feeling pretty triumphant myself. I felt like a new woman. By my standards (which were admittedly low), I'd done really well. I'd stood up to the Santini and lived. I could probably get into the *Guinness Book of World Records* for that.

We were still behind Carla and her entourage as we shuffled out of the auditorium.

"Look!" I pulled Morty's arm. "There's Lola and Sam."

They were standing together just outside the doors.

Morty and I both waved, but only Sam waved back. Lola was already marching toward Carla, her shawl flapping behind her and a murderous look in her eyes.

"Lordy, Lordy," muttered Morty. "I think we're about to find out why Lola missed the debate."

The Santini radar was still working. Overwhelmed by her own success and practically smothered by her supporters, Carla still clocked Lola before Lola could open her mouth.

"Lola!" screeched Carla. "Thank God you're all right." Her voice showed both relief and concern. She was acting her heart out. "We were all so worried when you didn't show up for the debate. I mean, it's not like you to leave Ella on her own like that. We were afraid something must have happened to you."

"Really?" Lola came to a stop, blocking Carla's way. Her smile was luminous. "How touching."

"I'm sure Ella will tell you all about it." Carla made a move to get past Lola. "You're in my way, Lola." She was still smiling. "I have a class to get to."

"Not yet, you don't," said Lola Cep. "You and I are going to have a little talk first." She raised her head for better projection. "Sam and I have a chilling, dastardly tale to tell."

In an almost unprecedented display of independent thought and action, Alma Vitters linked her arm through Carla's and took a step forward. "Come on, Carla," said Alma. "We don't have time for this crap."

Lola didn't budge. "But you do have time for kidnapping."

You have to hand it to Lola; she knows how to catch people's attention. Everyone had been edging around them, but now they slowed down or stopped. One or two even turned back.

"Kidnapping?" Carla shrieked with laughter.

In a perfect example of a chain reaction, Alma, Tina, and Marcia all started shrieking with laughter, too.

"Are you accusing me of *kidnapping* someone?"

Lola's look was haughty. She was doing her Dietrich. "I'm accusing you of kidnapping *me*," she replied. "And of tampering with my bike." Sam gave her a poke with his elbow. "And Sam's car."

"Oh, please. . . ." Carla looked so flabbergasted and sounded so genuine she could probably have passed a lie-detector test. "You know, you really should be on medication, Lola. The strain of living among normal people is beginning to show."

"You mean the strain of trying to act like a human is beginning to show in you," countered Lola.

Carla adjusted her books with a deep sigh. "Try to listen to me, Lola—and try to understand. I've been here since eight o'clock this morning, helping to set up the auditorium for the debate." She glanced at the coven. "Isn't that right?"

"That's right," said Alma.

Tina and Marcia nodded. Vigorously.

"And these are supposed to be independent witnesses, are they?" asked Lola.

"If you don't believe us, ask Dr. Alsop," cut in Alma. She was obviously practicing for the office of vice president. "We met him in the parking lot."

"And what does that prove?" demanded Lola. "You've never been one to do your own dirty work if you could find someone else to do it for you."

"You really are letting your considerable imagination run away with you, you know." Carla's sigh was filled with pity. "Just why do you think I'd want to have you kidnapped, if you don't mind my asking? It's not as though anyone would pay ransom for you, is it?"

"You know why you did it. So I'd miss the debate."

"You really do think the planet revolves around you, don't you?" Carla smirked. "In case you didn't realize, Lola, you weren't supposed to be in the debate. It was just the presidential candidates."

The coven sniggered.

"And let's get another thing straight," Carla went on. "If I did have you kidnapped, you wouldn't be standing here trying to make yourself look important." She started to walk away, but her eyes were on Lola like hooks. "You'd be halfway to Alaska by now."

Lola, Sam, Morty, Farley, and I all gathered on the lawn at lunch for the telling of the full chilling, dastardly tale of Lola's close brush with death and kidnapping.

"So anyway," Lola was saying, "there I was, bruised and shaken, pushing my bike along Rushmore Drive when this girl stopped and offered me a ride." She paused—as much for dramatic effect as to take her lunch from her book bag.

"A girl?" asked Farley. "What girl? Did you know her? Did she come from around here?"

"God." Lola sighed. "How I admire the scientific mind."

"Did you check the tire, Sam?" asked Morty. "Do you really think it was tampered with?"

Sam shrugged. "It's possible, but it's hard to tell."

Lola sighed again. "Am I going to get to tell my story, or what? I mean, it's not every day that I get kidnapped, you know."

"You seem to be taking it pretty well," offered Farley.

"I always try to be philosophical and see the good in the bad," explained Lola. "For an actress, being kidnapped is a priceless experience."

"I don't know . . ." Farley was shaking his head. "A flat tire could've been dangerous. Do you really think Carla would sabotage you like that?"

Lola, Sam, and I all answered at once. "You don't?"

Morty pushed his glasses back up his nose. "But it could've been a coincidence, couldn't it?"

Lola's laugh was shrill with derision. "Today of all days? You don't think that's a little unlikely?"

"Unlikely, but not improbable," said Morty.

Sam pointed his juice carton at him. "I'll tell you what's not only unlikely, but also completely improbable, and that's that I ran out of gas. I do not run out of gas. Not ever. Somebody drained my tank."

"So then what happened?" asked Farley.

"Well . . ." Lola put her sandwich down and looked at each of us in turn. "Then this girl in a Cherokee stopped and offered me a ride."

"And you took it?" Farley looked genuinely shocked. "Didn't your mother ever tell you not to take rides from strangers?"

"But it was a girl!" Lola protested. "She wasn't much older than we are. Who expects trouble from a girl?"

You'd think she'd never met Carla Santini, wouldn't you?

"So then what happened?" asked Farley.

"She said she had to stop somewhere before she took me home," Lola continued. "Only it took her a while to mention that that one stop was the mall. And then when we got there, she suddenly remembered a dental appointment, so she left me off—and that was the last I saw of her."

"Did you catch her license plate?" asked Morty.

Lola picked up her sandwich and slowly began to unwrap it. "Sadly, Morton, you weren't there to offer the benefits of your logical mind. And I was a little too wound up worrying about the debate to actually think about writing down her license plate number."

"It's not really very convincing, is it?" Morty has the indomitable perseverance of the born scientist. "I mean, you got a flat, you fell in the bushes, and you got a ride from some space cadet. You can't prove anything. It would never hold up in court."

"I wasn't planning to press charges," Lola informed him. "Anyway, it turned out that Ella didn't need my presence to defeat Carla." She smiled at me. "And all's well that ends well, isn't it?"

A dark shadow fell over our little group.

"Aren't you forgetting something, Lola?" Carla inquired politely.

Lola suddenly bit into her sandwich. "And what's that?" she asked through a mouthful of bread and cheese.

"It's not over till tomorrow afternoon."

It wasn't like me at all, but the truth was that I didn't give a hoot what Carla said. I'd been given a standing ovation. Now when I walked down the hallways of Deadwood High, people nodded, smiled, and said hello. A few even gave me the thumbs-up. For the first time since the election began, I felt that there was actually a chance (no matter how small) that I could win.

As far as Lola was concerned, of course, the election was already won. Which, as Sam said, was probably the only time in the history of the world that Lola and Carla Santini had ever agreed on anything. They just didn't agree on *which one* of us had won.

"Listen to her," muttered Lola in homeroom on Friday morning. She glared at the back of Carla's head. Carla was telling the coven, and everyone else in the room, what the first things she was going to do once she took office were. Lola snorted. "Talk about counting your chickens before they've hatched. She's not only counted them, she's decided how they'll be cooked."

"Carla's an absolute monarch," said Sam. "It doesn't occur to her that the peasants could ever revolt."

"Well, I hope they behead her," said Lola.

We decided to eat lunch outside to avoid any contact with Carla, but it was to no avail. Carla and her coven rooted themselves a few feet away from where we were sitting.

"I want to go through my acceptance speech just one more time," she announced loudly as they sat down. I could hear the smirk in her voice. "It has to be perfect."

"It will be," Alma assured her.

Marcia and Tina bleated their agreement.

The winning candidate's acceptance speech is yet another Dellwood High tradition: at the end of the last period, all of the candidates go to the office while the principal reads out the results of the election over the PA. Then the winner takes the microphone while the losers smile and pretend they don't mind.

Lola ripped her lunch from its brown paper bag. "Is she the most irritating person who ever lived, or what?" she demanded.

192

Carla heard her. She raised her head, cleared her throat, and started to thank her supporters. She sounded so warm and sincere that you'd think the words were coming from her heart and not the notebook on her lap.

Lola gave me a look. "You do have your speech, ready, don't you, El?"

I could feel myself redden. "Well . . . I mean, I didn't write anything down, but I kind of know what I'd say if I won." I should. I'd spent hours going over it in the bathroom last night.

"Not *if*," corrected Lola. *"When."*

Lola doesn't understand the concept of jinxing yourself because you're too confident.

Carla had moved on from thanking her supporters to thanking God when Sam turned up.

"What's Her Royal Highness doing?" He threw himself down on the ground between us. "It sounds like she's won an Oscar."

Lola scowled at her sandwich. "She's trying to bore us to death with her acceptance speech."

"Really?" Sam leaned back on his elbows. "It's too bad she's not going to have a chance to give it, then, isn't it?"

Lola and I looked over at him. He was smiling as if he knew where to buy a vintage Mustang in cherry condition for a hundred bucks.

"What?" hissed Lola. "What have you found out?"

Sam shrugged.

Lola punched him on the shoulder. "What?"

"Only that informal polls show a sharp drop in Santini supporters."

Lola and I said, "Really?" at the same time.

Sam grinned. "Really."

Sam had been talking to Morty and Farley. Morty had helped one of the running backs on the varsity team with his math homework, and this guy said that a lot of the boys thought Carla was way out of line. Farley's sister was a junior cheerleader, and she said her friends thought Carla had gone right over the top.

"Didn't I tell you?" Lola's shriek was pretty restrained, for her, but it caught Carla's attention. Without the slightest pause in her monologue, I saw one perfect eyebrow twitch.

I was excited by this news, too, but one of my jobs in life is being the Lola Cep reality check, so I tried not to show it. "That doesn't mean they're going to change their votes," I reasoned.

"No." Sam grinned. "But it means that they might."

"You know what I think?" Lola clapped her hands together. "I think we should have a party." She raised her voice to make it easier for Carla to overhear what we were saying. "We'll call it 'Good Triumphs over Ego,' and invite everybody." She grinned happily. "Except the Santini," she added more softly.

I'd sort of expected Sam to be his usual voice of reason, but I was mistaken. He didn't tell Lola she was crazy. What he said was, "Shouldn't we be generous in our triumph?" He smiled slyly. "I mean, what's the point in not inviting her? She isn't going to come."

"Maybe you're right." Lola tilted her head to one side, in the thoughtful pose of a serious president maker. "She's not Al Gore, is she? She isn't going to be gracious in defeat."

And it didn't look like I was going to be the voice of reason, either. I hadn't had a party since I was in junior high. I liked the idea. Especially a victory party. I'd never had a victory party, least of all celebrating a victory over Carla. I was still trying to hold on to reality, but my grip was loosening. "And where are we going to have this party?" I managed to ask.

Lola didn't bat an eyelash. "At your house, of course. It doesn't have to be elaborate. Just chips and stuff like that. As befits the party of the people."

"When?" asked Sam. "Next weekend?"

Lola shook her head. "No, tomorrow. That makes it more impromptu. You know, like a spontaneous gesture born of democratic joy."

"You mean so Carla doesn't have time to throw a counterparty," said Sam.

Lola winked. "That, too."

Lola, Sam, and I walked to the office with Morty and Farley that afternoon. Technically, Lola wasn't meant to be with us, but there was no way a mere technicality or even a teacher was going to keep her away.

"If Carla does win, the worst part's going to be having to watch her gloat," said Morty. "I'm really not looking forward to that."

Sam pulled open the door. "Try to look on the bright side," he advised. "If she does win, we'll probably have the chance to impeach her."

Carla and Alma were already behind the counter, standing near the microphone with Dr. Alsop, when we arrived.

"This election has taught me so much," Carla was telling Dr. Alsop as the four of us trooped in. "I feel I have a real understanding of the democratic process now."

"So do I," Lola murmured. "It's made me think twice about benevolent despots."

"Not me," said Farley. "I'm going with Sam. Anarchy's the only way."

"There you are!" Dr. Alsop looked pretty happy to see us. Which made one. Carla and Alma didn't so much as glance our way. "Come around here!" called Dr. Alsop. "It's almost time to start."

Sam, Lola, Farley, Morty, and I went around there. We lined up on the opposite side of Dr. Alsop from Carla and Alma. Small, insincere smiles were exchanged, but no words. Dr. Alsop didn't seem to notice that not all of the candidates were speaking to each other. He was so excited that he couldn't stop grinning. He wanted us to know how proud he was of all of us, and what a great job we'd done. He wanted us to know that even when he was older and grayer he would remember this election.

Carla said, "Dr. Alsop?" She held up her arm so he could see her watch.

"Right. Right." Dr. Alsop held up one hand for silence, even though he'd been the only one talking. "Everyone ready?"

We were all ready.

The microphone crackled. Dr. Alsop stepped up to it and launched into one of his mini-orations.

I concentrated on being calm. If when the winner was announced it wasn't me, I wanted to be prepared. Morty wasn't the only one who wasn't looking forward to watching Carla gloat. I was afraid it might provoke me to violence.

At last Dr. Alsop reached the moment of truth. "If we had an electoral college," he said, "the outcome of this election might have been very different. But here at Dellwood High School, it's the candidate with the most votes who wins." He cleared his throat. "In one of the closest races in the history of our school, the results are as follows . . ."

Lola squeezed my hand and I squeezed Morty's.

"Carla Santini, one hundred and fifty votes . . ."

"Way to go, Carla . . . ," whispered Sam.

I know it wasn't very mature, but I practically laughed out loud. One hundred and fifty votes meant that Carla had lost!

Lola squeezed my hand so hard I thought she'd broken some fingers.

"Ella Gerard, two hundred and twenty votes . . ."

I'm very good at mental arithmetic. Two hundred and twenty votes meant that I'd lost, too. Now I was breaking Morty's fingers.

Carla was staring at Dr. Alsop as though he'd turned into a giant lizard.

"Morton Slinger . . ." Dr. Alsop paused dramatically, ". . . two hundred and twenty-eight votes."

"That can't be right." Carla's whisper was a little shrill. "There must be some mistake . . ."

But it wasn't a mistake. It was the swing vote. The friends and would-be friends of Carla Santini who didn't want to vote for her hadn't voted for me—probably because they were afraid of what she'd do when they found out—they'd voted for Morty instead.

Lola, Sam, Farley, and I started clapping and cheering. Dr. Alsop extended one arm toward Morty.

"Ladies and gentlemen," he said, "It's with great pleasure that I hand over the microphone to Morton Slinger, the new student body president of Dellwood High."

Morty was still giving his first official speech as president when I slipped out of the office to call my mother from the pay phone outside. I'd already called her once that afternoon, but now I wanted to tell her the news— and to ask if she minded having the victory party anyway. "You don't sound too disappointed," said my mother.

"I'm not," I told her. "I feel just fine."

198

"Well, I'm not disappointed, either," said my mother. "Win or lose, I want you to know how proud I am of you, honey. I really am."

But there was one person who was disappointed, and she was standing right behind me as I hung up the phone.

I didn't have long to wonder how long she'd been there.

"Planning a party, Ella?" No one can make a question sound like a threat the way Carla Santini can.

I smiled. "Eavesdropping on other people's conversations, Carla?"

She smiled back as though I'd paid her a compliment. "You know, smugness doesn't really become you, Ella," Carla informed me. She sighed sadly. "I really think you've let this election go to your head. You used to be so much nicer . . . before . . ."

"Really?" I made my smile even bigger. "What a shame that I can't say the same about you."

"And you used to be more realistic, too." Carla shook her curls. "I mean, look at you, Ella. You're acting like you won, when in reality you lost."

"It isn't if you win or lose," I said. "It's how you play the game."

"Exactly," Carla purred. "It is how you play the game. And I'm playing this one so that you lose." Carla Santini's the only person I've ever known who can make a threat out of a smile. "Really, really lose . . ."

I stared through the glass wall of the office to where

Morty, Farley, Lola, and Sam were all shaking Dr. Alsop's hand. They all looked really, really happy. I didn't have to ask Carla what she was talking about; I already knew.

But despite what she said, Carla still thought she was dealing with the old Ella Gerard—the one who wasn't too good with subtleties. She explained what she meant. Maybe the student body of Dellwood High wasn't shocked and outraged by the news about my mother, but the people of Woodford would be. And Carla was going to make sure they found out. She was going to guarantee that my mother was socially ostracized. My mother would have more cold shoulders than an abattoir. She'd never cater for another party, attend another dinner, or be invited to another barbecue for as long as she stayed in Woodford. Which probably wouldn't be for very long.

"And what if Lola blabbed about Mr. Santini?"

"Now?" Carla's laugh was like funeral bells. "Who would believe her now? Where is her evidence? Where are her witnesses? Everyone would know it was just Lola up to her usual tricks."

I knew Carla well enough to know she was telling the truth. But Carla didn't know me at all. Not anymore.

Just a few days ago, I'd wanted to protect my mother. But now I was wondering what I'd been thinking. What exactly was I protecting her from? From losing friends she didn't really have? From missing out on a few boring dinners and barbecues? From catering for parties that weren't in Woodford?

All this time, I'd been standing in the phone booth, but now I stepped out, so there were only a couple of inches between Carla and me.

"You don't get it, Carla? Do you?" I looked straight into her eyes. "There's nothing you can do. You can get on TV and tell the whole world about my mother. It's not going to hurt her—and it's definitely not going to hurt me."

Carla laughed, but it lacked her usual overwhelming confidence. "So *you* say."

"That's right." I grinned back. "So *I* say." The Greeks were wrong after all. I really was lucky. I was lucky because I had friends I could count on. And I was really lucky because I could count on myself. "Because I won, Carla. And a lot more than a high school election." Now I knew that a person could do anything she wanted with her life—all she had to do was try. The trying was the important part.

"We'll see about that."

I could tell that for the first time since we were four and she said she'd break my new doll if I didn't give it to her that Carla was bluffing.

"Yeah, I guess we will."